CW00866265

FAMILY MURDERS

A Thriller

Henry Carver

Copyright © 2012 Henry Carver / FlashBang Books

All rights reserved.

This book is licensed under the Standard Copyright License,
and is a work of fiction. Names, characters, organizations,
places, and events are either the product of the author's
imagination or are used fictitiously. Any resemblance to
persons, events, or locales is entirely coincidental.

ISBN-13: 978-1493682195

ALSO BY HENRY CARVER

Sheep's Clothing

Ocean Burning

Bloodstained

"Happy families are all alike; each unhappy family is unhappy in its own way."

—Tolstoy

MONDAY

OCTOBER 8TH

1990

1

"AND THEN ROCKY knocked the cake out of my hand and he pushed me out of the way and ate it all off the floor. When he was done he came looking for more and licked me all over my face!" Julie giggled until it turned into full-blown laughter.

Angela Gray looked over at Rocky. He was a black and brown rottweiler weighing in at over a hundred pounds, and he was a rescue. By the time the Grays adopted him Rocky had already had three bad legs, the result of daily beatings. With time and care, two had healed. One never would. Some parents wouldn't let a dog like that near a five-year-old girl, but Angela had liked Rocky from the very first time she had seen him, trusted him even,

1

though she couldn't say why.

"At least Rocky's got good taste. That cake was delicious!" Ted Gray said, and started tickling Julie.

The fits of laughter and pointing must have clued Rocky in that they were talking about him, because he hung his head and looked at the floor, exactly like a person feeling bashful. He was what people call a dog with personality.

Every night at six-thirty the Grays sat down for family dinner. It was the one time of day they were all together. Ted worked long hours, but made it a point to be at the kitchen table by six-thirty because Julie would always go to bed not long after. Some people think that family is just a state of being, something static instead of dynamic, but being a family is an action. Family happens when families are together. Every night at six-thirty, sitting around the kitchen table, the Grays became a family all over again.

Angela loved this time of day, loved making the kind of family she had never had as a child come to life again and again. It was a hard thing to put into words.

"Another delicious family dinner," she said. "I love the three of you very much."

"Rocky too!"

"Yes, Julie, I love Rocky too. Now eat your peas."

Julie sneered down at her plate, and Angela was taken aback. Seeing that little face form new and adult emotions for the first time was strange. It was the first time she had seen Julie look at something with contempt.

"I hate peas! I want ice cream! Ice cream. Ice cream!"

Ted took up the chant now too. "We want ice cream! Give us ice cream!"

Angela laughed. "You too, Ted?"

Ted raised his hands and waited, melodramatically calling for quiet. Slowly, Julie's ice cream chant came to a halt and there was silence. It was a roomy pause, and even Rocky raised his head to look at Ted expectantly.

"Ladies and gentleman," said Ted.

"And Rocky!"

"Ladies and gentleman and Rocky, did anyone here read the paper this morning? No? Rocky, you didn't either?" No one said anything.

"I have an announcement to make. I, your humble husband and father, was in the paper this morning. I have been honored with the annual Garden Club award for best roses. Finally!"

Angela sat back in her chair. "Really?" Ted had been nominating himself into the competition for years, something she found to be a little childish. To be fair, though, their yard was immaculate. Even with all the hours he worked and all the business trips he took, Ted somehow found the time to be out in the yard almost everyday mowing and mulching, and above all pruning his rose bushes.

"Congratulations, Ted," said Angela, "maybe now you can spend a little more time with your family." She only managed to keep a straight face for a second, then Ted was hugging her and Julie was coming around the table to cram herself into the middle.

"Frankly," said Ted, "I think this might be the kind of situation that calls for a little ice cream."

"Daddy! Ice cream Daddy! Ice cream!" Between her birthday and the birthdays of classmates, long experience had taught Julie that the only proper way to congratulate or to celebrate was in the company of ice cream. Ted shamelessly took up the chant again.

"Ice cream, ice cream, *ice cream!*" When Rocky started in on the chanting, adding his distinctive baritone, Angela knew it was time to give in.

"Okay, okay. This calls for a real celebration. Tomorrow night, before Daddy leaves, we'll have a very special dinner. In the mean time, you animals stay here, stay happy, and I'll come back with some ice cream."

With days like this, one strung one after

another, Angela thought she could stay happy for the rest of her life.

2

SUPERMARKETS: THE MORNING brings the elderly, moving unmolested at a pace that could (with some charity) be called leisurely; the afternoon crowd is mothers and children, aisles clogged with strollers and saturated with crying; then comes the evening post-work rush, husbands picking up emergency milk standing in line next to bachelors stocking up on soup and TV dinners.

After that it quiets down, and after nine o'clock a supermarket is an abandoned, surreal place. It contains no people, just products, existing only as three-dimensional Warhol still-life, bathed in a halogen glow. It was, Angela thought, like working her way though a washed-out, remedial labyrinth.

She went up one aisle, down another, picking up this and that for the house. She hadn't seen another person since walking in. Even the checkouts at the front of the store hadn't been staffed. Wandering through the rows, where the bright lights obliterated all shadows and with them all relief, was like being alone on another planet. These lights were always glowing, day and night; there were no clocks on the walls; it seemed altogether a place unmoored from time. She had left the warmth of a happy family only ten or fifteen minutes ago, but here the emotional overtones were completely different. Overall, she didn't care for the supermarket at this time of day.

She turned the cart into the cool chill of the freezer aisle, trawling slowly along the frosted doors and looking for the strawberry ice cream. It wasn't in its usual spot. After a few more passes she saw it, up on the very top shelf in the middle of the aisle.

Angela opened the door, stretched, couldn't reach. She jumped up and brushed the carton with her fingers. Standing only a bit over five feet would make this tricky. She looked left, then right, and saw no one. Normally she would be too self-conscious to start shelf-climbing, but at this time of night, with no one else around, what choice was there? She braced a foot on the base of the freezer for her first step up.

"Need help?"

Angela's heart jumped, and on instinct she bounced out from behind the confines of the freezer door and spun around. There was a man behind her.

"Hey, sorry. I didn't mean to startle you," he said, "you just looked like you could use a hand."

It was strange the way he had appeared out of nowhere, but Angela told herself to loosen up and say something. "No problem. I just thought I was alone. I didn't even hear you coming."

The man smiled at her. He was at least as tall as the top of a supermarket freezer, and thin. He wore a faded t-shirt and corduroy pants over what looked like heavy boots. Angela couldn't place him in any normal mental category. The boots seemed heavy, like a something a construction worker would wear. The clothes were all surfer, tattered and casual, but he didn't have the tan—or the hair. What hair he did have was severe and dark, cropped close to his head and devoid of the bleaching effects of the sun.

All these were secondary observations to the most obvious one—his sunglasses. They were plastic wayfarers, the kind someone one a yacht might wear, and they were pink. That was the overriding impression: pink frames that drew attention to his face; dark lens that hid the eyes.

Here, under the harsh lights of the store,

Angela could easily see a shadow version of herself reflected in the lenses, but, somehow, she was having trouble seeing any real emotion reflected in his smile. He was standing very close to her.

"Can I give you a hand?" he asked, and the smile stretched a little farther. For a second, Angela thought he was hitting on her. Then, in the next moment, she wasn't sure. It was hard to get a read on him, and something seemed...well, Angela thought, what the hell.

"Sure," she said, "I'm trying to get the ice cream off the top. That's it, the strawberry."

"Ah, pink," he said, "my favorite. My sister's too. She loves this stuff." He handed her the carton.

"Uh, thanks."

"Hey, can I ask you something?" he said, and either took a half-step forward or just leaned in. Angela wasn't sure which. He didn't seem to move, just suddenly seemed closer.

"Can I ask you something?" he repeated, crowding her vision. "Gabe, by the way." He stuck out his hand.

She tried to shake without enthusiasm, but his hand was like a vise. "Gabe," he said again.

"Angela."

"Nice to meet you, Angela."

"Nice to meet you too."

"Say Angela, do you have a family?" He was

still gripping her hand.

"Excuse me?"

"I said, do you have a family? You know, like a husband? Maybe some kids?"

"Look," said Angela, "I appreciate you helping me out, but I'm not sure…"

"Maybe a daughter?"

Angela couldn't bring herself to say anything to that. She pulled back her hand. She didn't see Gabe move, but again he seemed closer. Even closer than before.

"The reason I ask is, I'm new around here. Actually, I'm not from around here at all, but I was thinking about moving here. You know—thinking about being new around here. What to you think?"

"What do I think?" she repeated blankly.

"What do you think about moving here? Is the area nice? What are the schools like? I have a family too—my sister. There isn't really anyone else in the picture, so I take care of her. I want the best for her. And I heard this area is nice. I heard it was full of nice people."

Angela looked at one lens of his sunglasses, saw one small, black reflection of herself looking back. She looked scared.

"If I moved here, maybe your daughter and my sister, maybe they could play together, right? How would that be?"

Angela was starting to feel exactly like her reflection: tiny and afraid. "How do you know I have a daughter?" she asked.

"Well, I asked if you did," Gabe said, "and you didn't correct me."

Her head jerked left, then right. Still no one around. This man wasn't touching her, wasn't holding her here in any way, but she felt trapped. Quickly, she started pushing the cart towards the end of the aisle, towards the turn where she would be able to see the check-out. Please, she said to herself, please let someone be there.

"Hey," she heard behind her, "I thought people around here were supposed to be friendly."

Please, please, please just let someone be there. She had that almost impossible-to-ignore feeling of something coming up from behind her, and the nearly irresistible urge to turn around.

Instead, she just kept moving, kept pushing the cart, unwilling to give in to a run. It was strange to feel the shake of adrenaline here in her supermarket, and as she rounded the corner she let out a sigh of relief. Under a lit-up, neon number four was an acne-faced high school boy staring off into space. Angela almost yelled for him, but decided not to give in to that urge either. She did allow her head a ninety-degree left turn, and took a long look back down the freezer aisle. No one there. Empty.

Abandoned again.

Checking out, Angela wanted to bring up what had happened, wanted to make some kind of report, wanted to ask questions, but in the end she didn't know what to say. Plus, she was fairly certain the boy wouldn't have any answers. Already the whole thing was starting to seem distant. Did I over-react? she wondered. Could it have been some kind of misinterpretation?

Pushing her cart out the door and into the open was difficult. She reassured herself with the fact that her car was sitting all alone. The parking lot was huge and empty, so she had a perfect line of sight in every direction. There was nowhere for someone to hide. Well, she thought, there is one place. He could be behind my car.

Behind the car. The closer Angela got, the more her cart slowed down. Finally, she was at a dead stop, standing under a lone streetlight and staring at the trunk. "Jesus, Angela, just do it," she said out loud, and with that she took three quick steps forward and stuck her head around the corner of her Celica.

Nothing. Empty black pavement split in half by the white line marking the edge of her spot. Cool night air filled her lungs and the adrenaline washed away, leaving her with something like a runner's high, and she felt like laughing. She filled the trunk with bags, got in, started the car, and pulled out of the lot. One hundred feet later, she saw the lights pull out behind her.

At first she couldn't believe it. Hers had been only car in the lot, but this car must have come from the lot too—the road had no other nearby entrances. She couldn't figure it out for a second, but then she had it. The employees must park somewhere, the acne-faced kid must have parked somewhere. Maybe behind the building.

Could this be him? The headlights got closer. Could this be some kid leaving after his shift? Angela made a left and held her breath. Just when she let the air out of her lungs, two beams slewed around the corner and attached themselves to the Celica's trunk. There was a high-pitched whining that could have been a gear shift, lower to higher.

She took a right into a subdivision. This was her alternate route home, the one she rarely took. No one was out this time of night, and the world was plenty full of subdivisions. It seemed a slim chance that some supermarket worker would just happen to live here of all places.

Or maybe not. Two headlights appeared behind her, two headlights with the same spacing, the same brightness. Angela realized the follower's brights were on. Even at this distance, they blinded her to any other details.

For some reason, the rudeness of that was her tipping point between fear and anger. She'd had enough, and gunned the engine for home. Get home, she thought, get safe. The headlights were still getting closer and closer, but the Celica's engine seemed maxed out. She couldn't go any faster. Up ahead was a familiar mailbox, and with a final twist of the wheel, her car turned down the driveway. She hit the brakes and threw it into park. And waited.

At the end of the drive a big engine slowed, then sped up, and two bright headlights flew past her down the road. In a few seconds Angela's heart stopped racing, and she started feeling foolish.

"Let's get this straight," she said to herself, "a guy talked to you in the store and then there was a car behind you on the road. Wow, sounds scary." She swallowed the lump in her throat, grabbed the ice cream, and went inside to her family.

TUESDAY

OCTOBER 9TH

1990

3

JULIE LOOKED UP from her asparagus. Earlier she had tried feeding it to Rocky, but even he wasn't having it.

"When is dessert?" she asked

"When you finish your vegetables, sweetheart."

Julie started to pout, then looked over at the counter and the cake Ted had picked up earlier today, a white one covered in pink roses he had thought would be appropriate. Angela watched Julie's eyes narrow and knew she was thinking it through, weighting the benefits of cake against the cost of actually eating her asparagus.

"Okay, Mommy," Julie said. She held her nose and started eating in tiny bits.

Angela looked around the table at her family—Julie already starting to think like a young woman, Ted looking at her too and grinning—and felt near total contentment. Her right hand jumped up to her chest, and she sighed.

"I love all of you." Julie appeared unmoved, completely focused on somehow managing to eat without tasting. Ted reached up and took his wife's hand off her heart. She hadn't told his about the store. The time had never seemed right.

"I love you too, Angela." His smile turned into a frown. "What about Klaus? Are you sure you two are going to be alright tonight without me?"

"It's just a storm, Ted," said Angela.

"It's a hurricane."

"No, they downgraded it, it's a tropical depression. But the only depression I'm going to feel is when you leave."

Ted groaned and Angela laughed. Sappy romance was one of their inside jokes. He squeezed her hand a little more tightly. "Don't kid about that. You know I hate taking all these business trips. I hate being away from here."

"Oh, sure, Ted. That's why you spent half the day mowing the lawn."

"Hey now, that's my 'me' time," he said. "Gotta get centered before something like this you know." Next to the door was a suitcase, garment bag slung

18

over it, ready to go. Ted was planning on cutting out of his own celebration dinner to fly to St. Louis.

"I just hope the partners appreciate how much you give up for them by doing these trips every other week."

"They do, Angela. And it'll come back to us. In spades. Someday soon I'll be here all the time."

"And who'll go to St. Louis for a short notice deposition?"

"Someone younger," said Ted, trying for grin. Angela laughed again.

"Now you're fishing for pity. Do you need me to say it? Okay, you're not that old."

"Daddy? Daddy is old. Daddy! You're old!" As always, Julie added her distinctive point of view to the conversation.

"Thanks, peanut. Alright everybody, I think that about wraps it up for me. I've got to get to the airport if I'm going to make this flight before the weather hits."

"Daddy, will you take me with you?"

Ted picked up his daughter. "Maybe I could just make you my carry-on, take you on under my arm, like this." With his other arm, he picked up his luggage and walked out the door. It was no trouble for a man over six feet with broad shoulders.

After he'd packed his things in the trunk, Angela and Julie stood next to the driveway and waved as Ted pulled out. He stopped on the street and called back through the open window.

"Save me some cake!"

Angela and Julie watched him head west, into the sunset. "Remember, Mommy, it's bad luck to watch someone out of sight."

"Yes," Angela said, "it is." They waited until Ted's sedan was a distant speck nearing the bend in the road, then turned and walked inside.

TWO HOURS LATER later Angela found herself shuttled between the darkness of sleep and the darkness of the world around her. One too many celebratory pieces of cake had induced an idea into her head, the idea that she should rest her eyes—just for a second. Angela got up at dawn every morning for a jog; late hours and cake were a dangerous combination. A jerking back and forth on her arm made her suddenly awake.

"Mommy. Mommy!" Julie was pulling on her, shaking her awake, but Angela couldn't see her. Her eyes were open, but the house was completely black. Angela's skin went cold. This was all wrong. At the very least, the photosensitive floodlights should be on at this time of night. She held tight to Julie's hand and pulled her into an embrace, her mouth close to her daughter's ear.

"Julie," she whispered, "why did you turn out the lights?"

"They just went out."

"What do you mean?"

"I was playing here on the floor, and there was a bang. A loud bang. The lights…they went out."

Rain lashed the windows, underscored by what sounded like thunder. But it was too consistent, too omnipresent, to be thunder. A flash of lightning lit the room, then another, revealing Rocky at the sliding glass door leading to the deck at the back of the house. He was crouched low to the ground, tail pointed down. Angela had never seen him like that, knew nothing about dogs, but understood instinctively that he was lowering his center of mass in a kind of preparation. His lips were pulled back, and the lighting flashed off his canines. The rumble Angela had heard was coming from his throat and seemed emanate in all directions. It was a visceral thing, a deep bass, that had the power to reach out and slide a finger across your internal organs. Instantly, she knew that something was out there.

She felt the tingle of adrenaline as it flooded her heart, then the tremble of cardiac acceleration. Without thinking she was up, off the couch, and backpedaling across the living room carpet, one hand still locked around Julie's wrist. Whatever was outside the door, Angela didn't want to know about

21

it—was prepared to forget about it—assuming it would just go away.

"You're hurting me."

Angela gasped, then shot her other hand out to cover her daughter's mouth.

"Quiet. You've got to be quiet. If you need to talk, whisper." Julie nodded. Angela dropped her and knelt to put her mouth close to her daughter's ear again.

"Mommy, Rocky's acting weird. He's been acting weird since you went to sleep."

"Do you remember when we talked about emergencies?"

Julie's eyebrows went up and her eyes widened. Her upper lip started to tremble. She grabbed onto Angela's arm and held on tight.

"Is this an emergency, Mommy?"

"I don't know, sweetie, but I think we should be careful, don't you?"

Julie nodded slowly, old enough to to follow the logic behind better safe than sorry.

"What do we do in an emergency like this, sweetie? When Daddy's not home and something bad happens?"

"We go to our rooms and hide, and wait for Mommy to come get us."

"That's right, Julie. Go to your room. Wait for me there. Don't make a sound." Angela pushed

Julie towards the stairs. Silent as a ghost she was up them, and gone.

Sending her daughter to wait alone in the dark raised the bile in Angela's throat. She'd spent too many nights like that during her childhood, waiting for her father to come home. Of course, sometimes she didn't hide. That was worse.

Thinking about her father transformed Angela's distress into outrage, and then into a kind of maternal fury. Her daughter was curled up under her bed, or buried in her closet, and whoever or whatever was at their door had caused it. Her hands clenched into fists. She stood up, faced the door, started forward.

"Easy boy. Easy Rocky." Angela ran her hand up through the short, stiff hairs on the back of his neck. Usually, when Rocky was riled up, she would grab him by his collar. Now her hand ran over it, past it, and came to rest on the top of his head. Her face was close to the glass in the sliding door.

It was dark out there. If there had been any lights in the house at all, Angela would have been staring eye-to-eye with her own reflection, totally unable to see anything else. Suddenly the darkness in the house seemed an advantage: she might not be able to see out, but at least no one could see in.

A bolt of lightning cracked across the sky and lit up the back yard. It was about an acre square, flat and lined on all three sides by stands of trees that reached back far from the house. The terrain seemed unusual to Angela, the yard somehow rougher than she had ever seen it. Out at the edge of the yard, something was moving.

Up. Down. Up. Down. It didn't seem like the movements of a person, but she couldn't see much. The edge of their deck was in the way, and Hurricane Klaus continued to spend itself against the glass. Some of the rain drops were moving sideways, some down, making a lattice that obscured her view of the yard.

Despite everything, Angela realized she was curious. Her hand went to the door handle. The other one got a firm grip on Rocky's collar, and then she pulled the glass open and stepped outside.

It was a shock. The rain hitting her in the face felt like hail, more solid than liquid. Rocky started pulling on her firmly. He didn't run; rather, he moved forward fluidly, purposefully, like a lion stalking his prey. Angela's hold on him was nothing more than a distraction, and in a few seconds he had pulled them to the edge of the deck. They were standing there, looking out, when lightning punched its thousand watt glow down into the yard.

Holes. Holes everywhere. The yard was covered with holes. In the darkness they had been impossible to pick out, nothing more than shadows, but for a second she could see that each one had a small mound next to it, a small pile of black earth. Rocky picked that moment to make his move. With one smooth movement he wrenched free of Angela's grip, leapt over the wooden bench surrounding the edge of the deck, and was traveling across the lawn like a shot, bad leg and all. He threaded his way between the holes, heading for a spot near the yard's rear corner. Angela stiffened in alarm and started down the deck's steps.

"Rocky!"

Rocky was barking, then snarling, then growling. Suddenly there was a yelp, but it was distinctly human.

Lighting flashed again. A figure, tall enough that Angela felt sure it was a man, stood dressed all in black. He was holding Rocky off with some kind of stick. Her worst fear was realized; someone was out here after all. Without thinking, her throat tightened into a shout.

"Rocky!" This time her scream found some momentary pause in the storm.

Man and dog both looked back at her. For a moment, everything was frozen. The dark figure dropped the stick, turned, and ran. There was a peal of thunder, and then the only evidence he was ever there at all were two swinging branches. Rocky stayed exactly where he was, triumphant. The threat was away from the house, so he stood still and continued to guard his territory.

Angela walked the last thirty feet to Rocky, to where the man had been standing. On the ground, at the edge of the woods, was a shovel. In the ground at her feet was a hole. Already, it was filling with rain.

She watched the water level rise. A plastic bag, lifted from below by trapped air, bobbed to the surface. She reached in, picked it up, turned it over. Though the mud and the water there was a glint of silver metal. It looked like a necklace, but she couldn't say for sure. It was dark and hard to see.

It may have been dark, it may have been hard to see, but just for a second—just before he turned and ran—Angela would have sworn the man had been wearing sunglasses.

Pink ones.

WEDNESDAY

OCTOBER 10TH

1990

4

"HE WAS RIGHT there."

Angela had one arm and one finger extended, pointing toward the back of the yard. Her other arm was wrapped tight around her chest, the first two fingers clutching a cigarette. She had quit smoking two years earlier.

"Mrs. Gray, I can understand why you would insist someone come out here. You're freaked out. Hearing that story, I'd be a little freaked out too. But look at it from my perspective—what exactly am I supposed to write down here?"

Frank Cooper looked at her from the other side of the deck, resting his pen and notebook on the knee of his brown flannel pants. His blazer was mismatched; his tie had the telltale signs of being slipped on each morning and off each night without ever being re-knotted. His hair was the same color as the overcast sky, unusual for a man who only seemed to be in his late forties. Most unusual of all, the eyebrows on his craggy face were still a dark brown. The mismatch was jarring.

"You're a detective, right?" Angela asked.

"I know that's what you asked for on the phone, Mrs. Gray," he said. "I suppose I could be considered a detective. Technically I'm the Assistant Chief, but that's just the title they made up to go with my position." He reached up and scratched his nose. "In a town this small, it used to be just guys in uniform and then the Chief, but a few years ago the population finally got to be big enough for there to be more substantial crimes."

"Substantial crimes. Like what?"

"Oh, nothing you'd consider serious after watching a little TV. We're talking small time robberies, check kiting, the occasional bit of insurance fraud. There's just enough of that sort of thing for it to be a good idea to have someone in charge of keeping an eye on it."

"So supposing you were a detective, you'd be the only detective in town."

"I'd say that's about right, Mrs. Gray."

"Call me Angela."

"Angela. Angela, you understand my problem, right?"

"No, I don't. He was right there." She pointed again. "He was digging holes all over the lawn. He was trespassing."

"Right, trespassing." Cooper raised his eyebrows. "This is a small town, Mrs. Gray."

"Angela."

"Right, Angela. But it's not that small. Do you really think they're going to detail me or anyone else to investigate a case of trespassing?"

"He threatened me in public, in a grocery store. He followed me home. Now he's coming onto my lawn and burying things. Wouldn't you call that something? Harassment?"

Cooper looked thoughtful. "I'd call it bizarre. Say for a second we find this guy and get his side of the story. Say he admits to it all. So what? Yes, sir, I talked to her in the grocery store. Then I drove home, happened to be going the same direction. No, sir, I've never been to the Gray residence. See where I'm going with this?"

"But he did dig up my lawn. He was here, I saw him."

Cooper started ticking things off on his fingers. "Firstly, it'd just be your word against his, even if we can find him. I'm not saying you're lying or even mistaken. But if I'm going to do anything at all, I need evidence." Angela glowered at him for a second, then turned to look out over the punctured lawn.

"Secondly, you said yourself that what you saw was a dark figure wearing similar sunglasses. No face, nothing definite. Is it a coincidence? I agree that it's probably not, but I can't do anything at all without evidence."

"What about cutting the power to the house? That's a hell of lot more than trespassing," she said.

"I had a couple uniforms check that out. It was a tree branch, took out the line. One of 'em even climbed the tree to take a look and the limb snapped right off, it wasn't cut through. It was a hurricane," he said, "or the last bit of one at least."

"What about the thing he buried?"

On the rough wooden table between them was the contents of the plastic bag, the contents of the hole. It was a short silver chain with a small locket attached to it.

"You don't recognize it?" Cooper asked, then picked it up and offered it to her.

"Should I touch it? Should you be touching it?"

Cooper grinned and kept holding the locket out. "Like I said, this is a small town. There's no one here with fingerprinting expertise, and expertise is what it would take to get something off this after the mud and the rain. That sort of thing is harder than it looks." Angela hesitated another second, then took it from him. Her fingers ran up and down the chain.

"No, I've never seen it before. It's for a child about Julie's age, but she doesn't have anything like it."

"Excuse me?" Cooper looked at her strangely.

"My daughter doesn't have anything like it," she repeated.

"May I ask how you know it belonged to a child?"

"I don't know if it belonged to a child, but it was made for one. Do you wear many necklaces, Detective Cooper?"

"Call me Frank. No, I don't."

Angela took the chain from Cooper's outstretched hand. "The chain is too short. Too short by far for an adult. I'd strangle myself just putting it on."

"Have you opened it yet?"

"No. I was waiting for it to dry, but I guess it's dry now," she said.

Angela tried to be as gentle as possible. The locket had a small hasp that she moved to the side, and a locking mechanism underneath that she pressed. The tiny container sprung open. Inside were two pictures, one on each side. The first was a young girl, about Julie's age. The second a young man, maybe high school age, sitting on the top rail of a rough wooden fence and smiling at the camera. The picture quality and the clothes they wore seemed about ten years out of date.

Angela showed the locket to Cooper. He looked at the pictures. "Anyone you recognize?" he asked.

"No. The boy looks a little familiar, but he's also a little generic. It makes me feel old old to say this, but all teenagers look a bit alike to me now."

"Wait until you're my age."

"So what happens now?"

"Nothing. I'll write a report. But there's no one to arrest, and there's not going to be an investigation into a report of trespassing. If you find more evidence, or…" he trailed off.

"Or if something else happens, right? Basically I have to wait for this guy to come back to get you to do anything."

"I'm sorry, Angela, but my hands are tied here. I wish there was more I could do."

"Look, I have to pick up my daughter from soccer practice. Where can I reach you?" she asked. He pulled a card out of his other blazer pocket. The card and the coat were about equally creased, like he didn't give out cards often and this one had been sitting on deck for a while.

"If anything comes up, here's my number. Call." He shook her hand and walked down the steps of the deck and around the side of the house to the front, avoiding holes where he found them.

Angela looked out over the expanse of the yard and considered her position, considered all the questions she had thought this meeting would resolve, now still swirling in her head. She was no closer to finding out who Gabe was, she was no closer to to figuring out why he was interested in her or her family, and she had no idea why someone would dig over a dozen holes just to bury a locket. Beyond simple craziness, of course.

She felt a shiver—whether it was the wind or something in her head she couldn't say—and dragged hard on her cigarette. That was what worried her the most, that he was just crazy. Then there would be no expectations, no way to predict what would happen next. No way to prepare for it.

She tried to remind herself that he hadn't seemed crazy. Real craziness was being terrified for your family, being terrified for your family with no one able to help. Angela had worked long and hard to build the life she wanted. If she had no help protecting it, fine. She would protect it herself.

She wasn't religious, and she didn't read the Bible. She didn't think often about the cosmic mysteries of the universe. But if there was a God, Angela felt sure of one thing: God helps those who help themselves.

5

EVEN THE SKY seemed threatening, desperate to unleash violence on the world below. Gray clouds bulged downward, pregnant with the possibility of storms to come. Having been through one hurricane already, Angela had to admit that living in anticipation was worse than living in the rain.

She had listened to the radio while driving to Julie's soccer field, and continued to listen to it while she waited in the parking lot. News of the next hurricane was on every station. Hurricane Klaus one day, now Hurricane Marco due just three days later. It was shaping up to be one of the most active hurricane seasons in recent memory.

Angela shook her head, shook off memories of the most recent storm, shook off the realization she'd had in the car: Ted wouldn't be home before this one was over. She'd called him at the hotel, but he was no longer staying there. It was a common occurrence. His law firm had contracts with lots of hotels in lots of different cities, and Ted would upgrade whenever he got the chance. She probably wouldn't hear from him until he got home. She did some mental math. No husband. No police. One stalker, one incoming hurricane, and only her to deal with the both of them.

As soon as Julie got in the car, that was it—she would be dropped off at school, picked up at school, and at home the rest of the time where Angela could keep an eye on her. Girls in cleats and shin guards began to pour around the edge of the bushes separating the soccer field from the parking lot. After a few minutes, the flow slowed to a trickle. By ones and twos and threes they climbed into the cars and vans surrounding her.

She had parked in her usual spot, right where Julie always found her, but after five or ten minutes it didn't matter. The other cars were all gone. Angela was lost in thought, but her head snapped up when she realized she was the only one left in the parking lot.

One moment she was mentally securing her daughter, already visualizing their reunion; in the next she had a feeling it was already too late. Panic was instantaneous and complete. Without realizing it, she was out the door and sprinting around the corner onto the field itself. The clouds were starting to open up again, dropping rain in her eyes. What would normally take only a fraction of a second dragged on forever. Angela was sure she was gone.

Then she saw her.

Julie. Sitting on the visitor's bleachers on the far side of the field. Julie, alive and whole. Julie, sitting next to someone.

A man.

A man in pink sunglasses.

"Julie!" It was a scream. Angela felt like she was flying across the field, somehow accelerating at her daughter without her feet ever touching the ground.

Julie's head snapped around, her face transforming from a smile into confusion. She stood up and started moving away from him, towards Angela, but slowly. So, so slowly. Angela couldn't take, couldn't wait another second.

"Julie, get away from him!" Julie looked back at the man on the bleachers. "Get away from my daughter!"

Then, she was there. Angela felt a flood of

pure, unadulterated relief flood her veins as she pulled Julie to her, squeezing her in her arms, but it left as quickly as it had come. Angela made herself let Julie go, pushed her back behind her body, and narrowed her eyes toward the bleachers.

"Who are you?"

"Look, I think there's been some kind of mistake—"

"I asked you a question. Who are you?"

In response he just reached up and took off the sunglasses. Until then he'd been doing a fair job playing surprised, but his eyes were smiling.

"Who the fuck are you talking to my daughter?"

"Mommy, that's a bad..."

"Quiet." Turning her head to shush her daughter, Angela became painfully aware of just how alone the three of them were. The field was abandoned, and she realized she was trading on pure bravado. "You get away from us. You get away and you stay away."

He put the sunglasses on top of his head and raised both hands in mock surrender. He really was smiling now. "Let me ask you something," he said.

"Julie, I want you to run to the car." She pushed her daughter in the right direction. Julie was unsure, but she starting walking. Then she stopped, turned, and waved.

"'Bye, Gabe!"

"'Bye, Julie." Hearing him say her name out loud was a nearly physical violation, like getting punched in the stomach. But Julie was gone, heading for the car, heading for safety. That was the important thing.

"Can I ask you something, Angela? Is your family important to you?" Gabe asked.

"If I was rude to you, or did something to you, then I'm sorry. But you need to leave me alone. You need to leave my daughter alone."

"I'll take that as a yes. And family is important to me too, Angela. How could it not be? Having something like that in your life, well, there's just no replacement. What would you do without your family?"

"I'm never going to find out. I'll never have to find out."

Up until now Gabe's expression had occupied a kind of crazy medium between smiling and sadness. Now his clear blue eyes, so often hidden behind black plastic, lit up. His hands clenched into fists. "My family was taken from me. So it was done, so it will be done to you. Get ready to feel my pain," he hissed.

She was in tears now, her gut turning over in mad disbelief. None of it made any sense. "Why are you doing this? Why? Why!"

"Because you're part of it. Don't you get it? You're guilty by association, and that's guilty enough for me."

"God damn it," she said, "what are you talking about? I'm not guilty of anything!"

As suddenly as it had come, the fire in Gabe's eyes sputtered and died. His forehead relaxed, his lips tightened, and his arm shot out. He grabbed her above the elbow and squeezed hard enough to make her cry out. Slowly, deliberately, he dragged her forward until they were nose to nose.

"You can serve up all the bullshit you want, Angela, but I've heard this one before. You live in that house, with that family, and you want me to believe you have no idea who I am? That you have no idea what I'm talking about?"

Angela pulled hard but her arm didn't move. She took a deep breath and tried to speak as calmly as she possibly could. "I don't know who you are. I don't know what you're doing here. If I did, maybe I'd understand what you're talking about."

Gabe's grip loosened and he took a half step backwards. His head tilted a few degrees to the left. For just a second, his resolve seemed to waver. Then the corner of his mouth turned up in a sneer.

"Almost had me going there. You're a good actress, Angela. I suppose you'd have to be, to keep up that perfect family front and live with him at the same time. You let him do what he does, you know."

"Let who do what?"

"He's a monster hiding in plain sight. And you're the decoration, you and Julie. You're the distraction. You're what he hides behind. Without you...," Gabe trailed off for a second. "Without you, he could never have lasted this long."

Angela looked around and confirmed they were alone on the quickly darkening field, Gabe ranting about someone who had wronged him, and admitted to herself that he might really be crazy.

"Look Gabe," said Angela, "we can try to get someone to help us figure this thing out. We can get help."

"Help is the last thing you deserve," he snorted. "What disgusts me the most is the girl. How can you let her play a part in this? She's so young. She's the same age as my sister. How can you live with yourself, knowing how close she is to him?"

"There must be some mistake. I really don't know who you're talking about. Why are you doing this?"

"Because I need you to do something for me. I need you to pass along a message."

Gabe let go of her arm, put on his sunglasses, and smiled. He turned and started across the field towards the woods on the far side. Five steps in he half-turned and called out.

"Tell you husband I say hello. Tell him I know where to find him and his family. And tell him I'll be paying you all a visit—very, very soon."

Then he was headed for the woods again, five steps, ten steps, more. This time, he didn't turn around.

6

ANGELA CIRCLED FOR what felt like hours, always looking in the rear-view mirror. Back in her own driveway, she sprinted from one car door to the other. She wrenched open the passenger side, grabbed Julie by the arm, and pulled her toward the house.

"Mommy, you're hurting me!"

"Come on, honey," she said, "we've got to get home." Her key was already out as they reached the front of the house, and then they were inside. The urge to simply slam the door was enormous. Angela felt like a kid again, hiding under the covers and waiting for her father to come home, totally unable to peek out. If she'd been alone, if she hadn't been a mother, this would have been the same. But for Julie's sake, Angela crushed down her panic, poked her head out the door, and looked.

Nothing. Just the gravel drive lined with trees and a dusting of the first fallen leaves rustling slightly in the wind. She pushed out a deep breath, hadn't even realized she was holding it in. Slowly, she closed the door and seated it in its frame as solidly as possible. Carefully, she twisted the small knob lock, shot the deadbolt, and slid the chain into its runner. They were secure. They were safe again.

She turned and pressed her back against the door. Her knees felt weak and she let herself slide down to the ground. It wasn't supposed to be like this. She had married Ted to make a life that was predictable and stable, to get away from anything like this. Sitting there, head between her knees, Angela thought she might start to cry. She lifted her head up and pushed hair out of her face, expecting to see her daughter worrying over her.

Instead she saw the empty foyer with all the lights off, sitting in silence. In the last light of an overcast day, openings into the dining room and the living room and the hallway to the kitchen all appeared cave-like, quickly receding into darkness.

"Julie!" Angela called out.

Nothing.

Fear gripped her again. Jesus, her own house,

her own safe place. Her house—the house she loved, the house she knew so well, the house that she had helped Ted design—was suddenly more terrifying than the world outside the door. Someone could be here, hidden somewhere, and there would be no way to tell. The place was full of nooks and crannies, crawlspaces and closets.

Angela's mind reeled under the force of a lurching shift in perspective. She had locked the door, thinking she would lock out danger in the process. Instead, she'd just locked herself into box with whatever might be lurking in here.

The urge open the door and run, to run and not look back, was overpowering. Some detached and objective part of her at the back of her mind almost laughed. How ridiculous to run into a house one minute and out of it the very next, and for basically the same reasons. Still, Angela thought, I could run. I would be running if it wasn't for Julie.

"Julie!" she screamed.

Again, there was nothing to hear. She could feel her right hand shake as she forced it out and along the wall, her fingers stretching toward the switch and finding it. For a brief second, Angela was convinced the power would be out again. She was afraid to flip it, afraid to find out.

She flipped it anyway. The light came on with a click. Nothing. Just an empty foyer, now harshly lit.

Some of the new light penetrated the doorways into other rooms, but the relative difference in illumination made the deeper parts of the house seem even darker than before. The end of the hallway in particular looked as though a dark curtain had been drawn across it. Angela knew the light switch was down there at the end. She strained to see it. As she looked, her eyes sensed something in the darkness. She could make out no detail, no edge. Just the barest hint of movement. And then a tiny bit of color.

A tiny slice of pink.

A black shape exploded through the curtain of darkness, coming fast and low and right at Angela's heart. Adrenaline catapulted outward from her core down to the tips of her fingers and toes. Instinctively, she pushed backwards. The edge of the small carpet there caught her heel. She fell, and knew it was over before she hit the floor. There was no more time.

Angela gave in. She closed her eyes tight, pulled her arms around her, and waited for it to happen. A hot, rough tongue scraped itself across one side of her face. She opened the now moistened eye and saw Rocky, tongue out, smiling at her.

"Rocky!" she said, and started to laugh. Once it started it was uncontrollable, like all the energy reserves her body had summoned couldn't be put back into storage. The cannon fuse was lit, the firework was already soaring towards the sky. Now it had to shoot, to explode, to get out—one way or another. Angela was laughing, a deep and free belly-laugh, laughing so hard snot ran down her face. Rocky licked it off, which only set her off harder, faster. She couldn't breathe.

Julie.

One word chilled the hot fire in her belly to ice water, but strangely, she didn't panic this time. The jitters were gone, the nervous energy vaporized like flash paper in a flame. She felt collected and clear-headed. Instantly, she knew what to do.

"Rocky! Go find Julie!" The dog pitched his head sideways, questioning. "That's right, Julie. Where's Julie? Find her!"

Rocky gave one of his distinctive barks, a kind of bellow, then turned and ran, nails clicking across the hardwood floor. Angela felt a primal joy in their new approach. She and Rocky would hunt Julie down and protect her, and that was that. Freed of her fear, she charged after the big dog. She didn't turn on any lights as she went, sacrificing vision for speed, trusting Rocky to lead her. She turned a last corner and found him sitting at the end of the other hall. He was facing an unstained pine door, a door that was always closed and locked.

A door that was hanging a few inches open.

Coming up to it, Angela could feel a draft of cold air setting her hair on end. Beyond the door lay the addition Ted had insisted on. It would add another thousand square feet of elegant space to the house, he'd said. Right now it was anything but elegant, just a rough wooden floor with a frame built up around it, tightly wrapped in huge sheets of plastic to protect against the elements. And it was empty. Ted didn't feel comfortable with workers alone in a house with two girls, he'd said. No telling what could happen while he was away.

No telling at all.

She pushed on the door and felt resistance. All the cool she had collected started to drip and drain away. Her muscles tensed and she pushed harder. The door slid open, tipping back the sandbag that had been leaning against it. Rocky pushed past her legs and into the construction area. Angela followed him.

Standing near a big gap in the floor, looking down, was Julie. Without thinking, Angela was there. She had no memory of moving from one place to another, just of kneeling behind Julie and locking her arms around her.

"Mommy was so worried about you, Julie," she said, "didn't you hear me calling? What are you doing in here, sweetheart?"

"I heard something, Mommy. I was looking for

Rocky, just like when I get home everyday. I heard him in here. Or just maybe I did."

"What are you doing near the hole to the new basement?"

"That's where he was when I heard him. Now he's up here!" Julie laughed and gave her dog a hug.

Once again Angela had the unmistakable urge for flight, to take her daughter and run. But she'd come this far, and next to the gap in the floor was one of those yellow construction lights. It was on a stand, with a metal grill over it to prevent things from falling in and burning, and it had a handle hooked across the top near a big on/off switch. Angela reached down and picked it up. She shuffled towards the edge of the hole, angled the light, and flipped the switch.

Nothing. Once again, Angela found herself protecting against the shadows.

"How did you get in here, sweetie?" she asked.

"When I heard…I just came in, Mommy."

Angela swept the light from side to side, up and down. "Where did you get the key to open the door?"

"Oh, the door." Julie cocked her head the side. Rocky mimicked her. Angela kept scanning back and forth with the light. "The door was already open, Mommy."

And there they were. Far back right corner, propped upright, facing out, displayed, just waiting to be found. A pair of pink plastic sunglasses.

In the heat of the moment, realizing how close Julie had come to something, Angela dropped the light. It fell down into the hole, rolled, and sputtered out like some medieval torch. Wordlessly, she grabbed Julie and headed back to the regular house. Rocky sensed their direction and was through the door before they were. Back in the house, Julie pulled the door shut behind her, just like she had been taught. There was a key to lock it, but Angela didn't know where it was kept. They never used this door. She settled for pulling the hallway table in front of it. The door opened outward, and the table was covered in vases and glass figurines. As a compromise (and as an early warning system) Angela figured it wasn't bad. Plus, she thought, they had Rocky.

A ringing came from other room. The phone.

"Stay with me, Julie. Come on Rocky." Together they headed for the kitchen. She paused in front of the phone, then picked up, cutting it off mid-ring.

"Hello," she said neutrally.

"Hello, I'm trying to get in touch with Angela Gray."

"This is."

"Mrs. Gray, this is Detective Frank Cooper. From the other day." She said nothing, and he must have detected something in the silence. "Angela, what's wrong?"

"Jesus, Frank, you've got good timing," she blurted out.

"What's going on?"

"There was someone in the house. And I saw him again, the man in the sunglasses. He's was here. He was here!"

"Slow down, just tell me what's happening."

Suddenly hyper-aware of the house's negative space, and unsure of what could be filling it, Angela realized that shouting was only marking her position. She downshifted to a whisper.

"He's here. Or he was here. And he's after my family, Frank. Not just me. Ted. Julie. He found her alone on a soccer field not an hour ago."

"Angela, I don't care about an hour ago. I care about what's happening right now. You're sure he's in the house?"

"No—but he could be."

"I'm sending someone right over. But it will take a few minutes."

"How many minutes?"

"Maybe five." Frank sighed into his mouthpiece. "Probably ten. Rush hour. The weather. I want you to take Julie and hide.

Somewhere you can fix the door so no one can get in."

Angela swallowed. It made sense, just hide out and wait for someone to come. The master bedroom would be the best place. Without lingering any longer she grabbed Julie and swung her up and across her chest and started running. Through the hall, cutting the corner off the foyer, turning up the stairs, a hard right into the bedroom.

The bed easily accepted a thrown child. She slammed the door and twisted the small recessed lock. The phone went back to her ear as she caught her breath. She imagined Frank Cooper sitting in an office, surrounded by cops, cops with guns, listening to her gasps. It was a comforting thought, somehow. If anything happened to her, everyone would know, and if anything was about to happen Angela would make that very clear. She could hear herself now: "I'm on the phone with the police right now! You better get out of here, asshole!" She almost laughed again.

"Angela, are you still there?"

"Yeah, we're in the master bedroom. The door is locked. I think we're okay."

"Look, I don't want to alarm you, but I want you to open the closet."

Angela felt a spike in blood pressure.

"I know how that sounds. I couldn't have you

and the girl walking around checking the whole house. But you had to go somewhere, and that place we are going to have to check."

She said nothing.

"We'll do it together."

Cooper's voice sounded tinny and distant, distilled though cheap government electronics. Angela was suddenly finding far less comfort in something as ephemeral as an open phone line.

"You're not here, Frank," she hissed.

"Just do it, Angela."

Unconsciously she had turned and oriented herself to face the slatted closet door, and now she was backing away. Some part of her knew anyone in there could be looking out at her right now, listening to everything she was saying. It was the same part of her that winced even before a needle actually went in her arm. Now it made her close her eyes for second and wait for the inevitable: the snapping of thin, pine slats; the obliteration of a fragile latch; the outward explosion of the closet door as he came for them.

Angela cracked an eye. The door was still whole. It was just sitting there. That, at least, seemed reassuring. She made herself walk forward, clutching the cordless handset like some kind of club. In the end she did it just like ripping off a band-aid. One quick motion, one jerk of her arm, and the door was open. Clothes. Shoes. Boxes.

Nothing. For what felt like the hundredth time, Angela felt tension melt down through her toes and into the floor below. She wasn't sure she could keep doing this, ratcheting herself up only to bottom out.

"Frank, there's nothing in the closet. I think we're okay."

"What about the bed?" he asked.

It turned out she couldn't keep doing it after all. With a grunt she turned and charged the bed. The idea that Julie could right this second be sitting eight inches over his head was too much. Without thinking, Angela stuck her head into the dark space. She didn't find anything this time either.

"We're fine, Frank. There's no one here."

"OK, good. Sorry about that. Old habits, I guess."

Angela's annoyance at taking direction faded. "That's alright. It was the right thing to do. How long until someone gets here?"

"It's only been a few minutes."

"Feels like longer. Feels like things are stretching out over here."

They both sat in silence for what felt like a while. Angela was sure now that her perception of time was being distorted, sure that it was really only seconds.

"Just talk to me," she said. "You keep talking

and you'll keep me talking. That will keep me from thinking."

"What should we talk about?"

"Why did you call me?"

"I think you picked the wrong subject."

"It's about him, right?" Cooper didn't say anything. "I know it. I can hear it in the way you're breathing. One way or another, you called about him. Who is he?"

"I don't know who he is. I did call about the case, but it was about the locket," Cooper said.

"The locket he tried to bury in my back yard?"

"Yeah. I had a couple people take a look at it. Found out a couple of things."

"Like what?"

"Well, the bag. The plastic bag it was in? It was heat sealed. One of our evidence techs says the way it was done was pretty fancy in and of itself. Anyone can melt plastic together, but normally that weakens it. The point of a professional heat sealer is just that—it makes a good seal. They can tell a little bit about the quality of the seal. How good it is, how expensive the machine is."

"And?"

"And it's pretty high quality. He says the sealing marks indicate it's not an industrial machine, so it must be a one designed for home use."

"And you can figure out who owns one of these machines?"

"Um, no, there's no way to find that out. We'd have to call all the companies, collate all the customer lists, and then what? Visit them all? They could be all over the country."

Angela stayed quiet.

"I don't want you to think...I want to help," Cooper said, "but we're a small department. I know this guy is harassing you. Starting now we can have someone keep an eye on the house." He paused. "But as far as finding the sealer, the department is only going to give that kind of treatment to a real red ball. A manhunt or something."

"So you called to tell me you can't find the guy."

"Not exactly. My point is, the bag was sealed when you found it. There were no rips or holes."

"No."

"That's because the plastic was thicker than someone might normally use. Tough, durable. This guy went to a lot of trouble to protect the locket from the elements." He paused as though this spoke volumes, begging the question.

"But?" Angela asked.

"But there's dirt in the locket."

"Dirt?"

"Yeah, dirt, in the grooves and in the etching. If

there's dirt in the locket, it must have come from before he tried to bury it, from wherever this guy was when he sealed the bag up. Either where he lives or where he works. Something. But he cared about the thing, enough to take care of it at least, and he handled it a lot, at least it would seem so from the way dirt was ground down into all the cracks. He practically fondled the thing."

"But it couldn't just be dirt from being buried."

"No, the bag was sealed. You said it yourself, when that hole filled with water it popped right to the surface. It was filled with trapped air. And if it's airtight, well, then it's definitely dirt-tight too. The dirt came from wherever it was before."

"And dirt's going to help you find someone," Angela said skeptically.

"Believe or not, yeah. People expect something like fingerprints in every crime, but they're pretty rare. Most things you touch won't show a print, and most times you touch something smooth like glass you smear your own print away. But dirt—dirt gets everywhere. It adheres to shoes and clothes and under fingernails."

"But dirt's dirt."

"Not really. It's a geology thing, but most dirt is pretty unique. With some expertise and copies of the county geological survey, it can be linked to some pretty specific locations. That's what we're going to try to do."

"That sounds like a lot of resources. The resources you said the department can't waste."

"Well," he said, "it's no manhunt, that's for sure. It may be a bit of a job, but it's a job that can be accomplished by one person."

"One person?"

"Yeah. Me. God knows, I've got the time."

"Thank you, Frank. Really. I know you're taking a personal interest in us."

"If you don't mind me saying, I like you Angela. But more importantly, and not to make light of your situation, I like a good brain teaser. I don't have to do much thinking here in semi-retirement. Come to find I miss it at least a bit. I'll find out what I can."

The sound of crunching gravel came from the driveway. Angela took her back off the door and walked over to peer out the window. A black and white sedan was pulling to a stop in front of the house.

"Frank, the squad car is here."

"That's good. See? Everything's going to be fine."

"What was the second thing?"

"Excuse me?"

"You said you found out a couple of things. What was the other one?"

"We can finish up right how if you want. I've probably taken up too much of your time."

"Right now, I need you to keep talking."

"Look, I don't want to upset you, but I'm not just looking into this case as some kind of favor. There's more to it than that," he said. "We know where the locket came from."

"Wait, now you know where he is?"

"It's not that." Cooper paused, seemed to be collecting his thoughts. "You had a weird story, Angela. I told people here at the station about it. Showed a bunch of them the locket too. One of the cops, one who's been here a while, he recognized it. It's something that went missing." He paused again. "We think it might be a piece of evidence in another crime, one that happened about ten years ago."

"What kind of crime?"

"That's not important. What is important is seeing if we can connect this locket with someone. It's important that we find, er, Gabe."

Angela felt some bile rising in her throat. She liked the older detective too, but this was too much. "I'm being harassed, threatened, and you told me there was nothing the police could do. But now you're going to try to solve some ten year old crime instead? I'm here, right now! I need help, right now, and you're trying to close out some ten year old burglary?"

"I'm afraid we really do have a responsibility to investigate this."

Angela was shouting now. "Just help me, Frank! Why are you possibly doing anything else?"

"Because it wasn't a burglary. It was a murder."

That shocked her into silence.

"And when we get information about a murder, we have to run it down. I'm going to help you, Angela. I just want you to understand—we have to do this too."

"Did they catch him?"

"Excuse me?"

"Did they catch the person who did it?"

"I think that would be an upsetting subject. We don't need to get into it."

"Do you think I know something about it?" she asked.

"Not at all. I just want you to understand what's going on."

"Who was murdered?" Angela took a deep breath. "And did they catch whoever did it?"

"Yes and no," Cooper said.

"Jesus, just tell me."

"Someone was arrested, yes."

"And what happened to him? It's a him, right?"

"Yeah, it's a him."

"And?"

"And the trial didn't go well."

"I've never been at a trial, Frank. What does that mean?"

"It means a not guilty verdict."

"But he did it?"

"Well, the police who worked the case thought so. The district attorney who took the case thought so too, and that means a lot. DA's don't like to lose—bad politics. I've seen plenty of cases where it was a sure thing the guy did it but the evidence was weak, and the DA would let the person walk. No trial, no nothing. The evidence was weak in this case, but, ah, I guess the DA must of felt pretty strongly about it."

Angela thought for a moment, then asked another question. "What does that mean? Why did he go out on a limb for this case?"

"Well, he had his reasons. I spent the last few hours reading the file, and most of everyone's time was spent looking for something. Something that should have been there but wasn't. Kind of a Sherlock Holmes thing, you know? The dog that didn't bark and all that."

"What was missing?"

"A locket," Cooper said.

"My locket."

"Yes."

Angela thought about it. She sat on the edge of

the bed, cradled the phone between her shoulder and ear, picked Julie up and sat her on her lap.

"But it's not my locket, Frank. Something like that, the ownership speaks for itself. Can't you figure out who's in those pictures inside?"

"We know who they are. They're brother and sister. The boy is the one who went on trial."

"And the girl?"

Cooper hesitated. "The girl?"

"The little girl, what about her?"

"It's a terrible thing, Angela. The little girl is the one who was murdered."

THURSDAY

OCTOBER 11TH

1990

7

THURSDAY, DOWNTOWN IN the big city. It was the lazy late afternoon time when the streets are deserted—after all the lunch-goers have finished up, but before office workers start ducking out early trying to beat the rush hour. For about ninety minutes, the world seems abandoned.

Angela paused at the base of the worn stone steps, pulled her coat closer around her neck, and turned in a full three hundred and sixty degree circle. She did it slowly, reaching out not only with her eyes but with her instincts, probing each alleyway, searching and hunting for the barest hint of pink.

Nothing. No one. There was no place to hide,

no crowd to blend into. Angela decided she was, at least for the moment, alone. Being alone meant being safe. She turned and ascended the steps to the library.

Inside it was warm. She wandered left, then right, looking for the right desk and the right librarian, mentally checking all her steps along the way.

Julie had been invited to a sleepover with a new friend. It was good news, and unexpected. As bubbly as she was in the Gray house, outside of it Julie was quiet, even shy. She didn't make friends easily, so a new friend was always welcome. More importantly, she had never been to this friends house before—it wasn't part of any routine. Angela had driven Julie over herself, and had seen almost no other cars on the trip. The ones she did see were all headed in the other direction.

All in all, she was fairly certain that, as of this moment, no one could know exactly where Julie was. The difficulty had come in persuading herself to accept a simple truth that she'd internalized long ago as a very young and very scared little girl: sometimes kids are safer far, far away from their parents.

With Julie safe, she'd headed for the nearest big city. It only took a few hours of research for her to realize that local journalism wasn't reliable. Even worse, it wasn't archived. At their local library, ten year old copies of the local paper existed only in hard copy, box after box of them stored in a damp basement. The boxes were only loosely chronological, stacked in order until space ran out, and then stacked again somewhere else. There was no rhyme or reason to it, no index or cross-referencing, and no way to find articles by subject or byline.

She had quickly given up. Seeing the look of defeat on Angela's face as she came out of the basement, the local librarian had offered a piece of advice and an explanation involving the press wire and the idea that the same stories are printed in bigger papers, papers with a more progressive attitude toward archiving yesterday's news.

All of which had lead her here, to the nearest city anyone would venture to call big. The story she was looking for had itself been big on a local level; it hadn't been big enough to get any kind of national coverage, but it had been big enough to draw in reporters on assignment from the surrounding area. Angela was sure she would find what she was looking for. She could feel it.

Detective Cooper had ended their phone call soon after realizing he had said too much. Angela thought he really did care about her, that he was only looking our for her best interests. He thought the idea of a little girl, so close to Julie's age, murdered, would terrify her.

And he was right—she was terrified. But so much of the fear she had felt at that moment was the fiery desire for safety, to survive. This was much colder. She was resolved. One way or another, there had to be an answer about what was going on, about what it all meant. And she was going to find it, with or without the help of the police.

Cooper had only yielded one more small detail before hanging up, but it was the most important one of all, a name. It made the search so much easier. Angela approached a librarian sitting at a desk set back behind the stacks.

"Excuse me, I'm trying to find a group of old newspaper articles all pertaining to one subject."

"What's the subject?"

"A murder. From ten years ago. November 1980."

"Do you know the name of the victim?"

"Gabrielle Fallows."

After that it was easy. News doesn't stay current forever. Stories have waves of popularity, so nearly all the articles were grouped around the time of the murder and arrest, and then again around the time of the trial. They were on microfilm, but the librarian was more than happy to pull the appropriate rolls and set Angela up at a reader in a back corner.

At this time of day the library was nearly as empty as the streets outside, so there was no one to hear her gasp when she saw his face. It had only taken a few twists of the knob and there he was, much younger, but already in possession of that lean and handsome face.

"Gabe," Angela said under her breath.

There was no question he was the boy in the locket, but he looked so different now. It was the eyes, she thought. In the newspaper picture he was being pushed toward the open back door of a boxy sedan. There was a caption underneath: *Eric Fallows, the primary suspect in the rape and murder of his younger sister, Gabby Fallows.*

"Jesus Christ." Whatever she had expected—an accident, negligence, coincidence—an incestuous pedophile sex murder wasn't it. Somehow she had thought the locket and its owner would be just the first clue in a long line of clues, part of a chain. But here was the connection, immediate and plain as day.

Eric Fallows. Gabe had never seemed like the right name, but this explanation was far worse than she could have ever imagined. Masculinizing and taking his own dead sister's name, the seven-year-old sister he had raped and murdered, seemed inexplicably sick. The thought of Julie sitting alone

71

with him on a soccer field made her want to throw up.

The coverage was extensive. She had never heard of the case, but she wasn't from here. This was Ted's home town. They'd met while Angela was still in college and had moved back after Julie was born. Ted thought a small town was the right place to grow up. He'd never mentioned anything about this, but ten years ago would have been just around the time he had left himself. It was good he'd held back—knowing it now was hard enough.

For just a second, it seemed like enough. This was what she'd come for, to confirm or deny the lead that dropped into her gut every time she conjured up his smiling face. And here it was: confirmation. He was everything she thought he could be and more. Much, much more.

"I could leave now," she thought, and almost did.

Instead, she started reading. She read for a very long time.

8

IT WAS A Tuesday—November 11th, 1980. At just before four in the afternoon a call to 911 was placed by a person, later determined to be eighteen-year-old Eric Fallows, reporting the discovery of a body. Even then the town was small, and with nothing so big as a child murder to attend to, having not seen a murder in the previous ten years, the police—all of them—came as quickly as they could.

They found Eric Fallows covered in blood and catatonic, cradling his sister's body and sitting in a rocking chair on the front porch of his house. In early stories the details of the actual crime were sketchy, presumably the result of a small town's police force attempting to preserve the dignity of its citizens. It was reported that some veteran officers refused or were unable to approach Eric on the porch in his condition. Some threw up.

Eric was sent to the hospital, riding in an ambulance along with his sister's body. He started talking during the ride, insisting that he be taken to the police station so he could tell them who killed his sister. Officers met him at the hospital's front door, then took him to the station. Despite their strong advice that Eric wait until they got there to tell his story, both patrolmen heard it twice during the car ride. Eric was starting in on a third telling as they arrived. Once in an interview room he repeated the same story again and again—for detectives, for lawyers, into microphones, to anyone who asked, for anyone who would listen. He would repeat it for the last time at his trial.

The evidence against him was strong. A cursory search of the house turned up the murder weapon, a filet knife sitting in plain sight on the kitchen counter. It was part of a set that belonged to the house, and the blood on it was Gabby's. Two fingerprints were recovered, and they corresponded to Eric's right index finger and thumb. As far as detectives could tell, she had been assaulted and killed in her own room, then dragged down the stairs and out onto the porch. Some of the wounds were deep and violent enough to suggest the strength of a larger male. But if Eric had the power to carry the body then he could have inflicted the damage too. He had access to the knife and he had touched it, and he had been all alone in the house with his sister. It was clear means and opportunity.

As far as motive was concerned, semen recovered during the autopsy told detectives all they needed to know. Once it was typed and found to be the same blood type as the victim's brother, most of the police working the case started closing up shop, calling it a day. In the span of twelve hours Eric Fallows moved from potential witness to suspect to certain murderer.

As it turned out, there were no witnesses. The Fallows lived on a farm. The whole area was rural, but their piece of land particularly so, with a half-mile gravel drive and a house shielded on all sides by poplar and birch. Only Eric's word stood against the damning facts of the case: the blood; the murder weapon; the body. Besides, he was the only suspect. There was some speculation about why then he would call 911 on himself, but the average response from both government officials and the writers of editorials amounted to this: if you're crazy enough to rape and murder your own sister, then you're crazy enough to do a lot of things.

There was rampant speculation at trial about psychopathy and sociopathy and many other pathologies, including the influence of the horror genre and movies like John Carpenter's Halloween, which had come out only two years ago at the time. Whatever the spin, everyone agreed he was crazy. No one would say it in court—people were hoping for an execution—but there seemed no other explanation.

Two things counted toward a conclusion of sanity.

One, a lot of people had know Eric Fallows for a long time. He had always been considered a shy boy, but upstanding. By all accounts he had been devoted to his sister. The father was a lush, the mother long gone, and in many ways Gabby was the only family the boy had ever had. Though there seemed no other explanation for her death, most God-fearing local people prided themselves on being able to recognize evil, and resented the idea of being hoodwinked all these years by one of their own. Some flat-out refused to believe it.

And two, Eric Fallows never once wavered in his story. In all the tellings he gave of it—and between the cops and the lawyers and the press there may have been hundreds—details, small details, were always the same. Perhaps he had spent his supposed catatonia constructing a tale that would exonerate him, but to be unhinged enough to commit the crime and yet collected enough to fabricate the story seemed almost too terrible to contemplate. It implied a person who knew exactly what he was doing, while he was doing it, a man who enjoyed his work. Certainly he enjoyed the murder (in later articles it was described as a "sexual frenzy") and now he was putting as much flair and theatricality into his defense, joyfully pulling the wool down over they eyes of an entire town.

His story was this: the elder Fallows had been out of town for some time. Everyone described this as less than unusual. Gabby was in second grade, and every day she would be dropped off at the end of the driveway by a school bus at around two-thirty in the afternoon. Her routine was that she would walk the last half-mile to the house and then take care of herself for between ninety minutes and two hours, depending on when Eric would get home. He worked part-time as a welder and would usually be back by four-thirty at the latest.

On Monday, November the 10th, one day before the murder, a small gas leak was discovered in the welding shop where Eric worked. The shop was cleared out and the foreman started questioning employees because a gas leak would cause problems with permits. The facts pointed to one veteran employee, who insisted the work in question had been performed by the new guy, the kid, and pointed to Eric. Words between Eric and the foreman became heated. He wouldn't admit any fault, said some things he shouldn't have, got fired. Later, after the case was under way, the veteran employee admitted it had been his fault while being questioned by detectives. Eric had been telling the truth.

Those events added up to Eric walking home just like on any other day, only about two hours earlier. He walked home and was at the end of his driveway by two forty-five, half-expecting to run into Gabby there. In fact he did run into her, but she wasn't alone. In Eric's story, someone else was there too.

Eric said he had turned the corner and seen a cherry-red, two-door Dodge Challenger, idling, sitting halfway between him and the house. It was pointed down towards the street, and as he got closer Eric could see Gabby through the windscreen. She was sitting low, nearly swallowed up by the leather of the passenger seat, but he could see her face. She looked scared. Then came the soft grind of gears meshing as the transmission fell into first.

There's no way to tell what might have happened in a given situation, only what did happen. Eric was always adamant the car was about to take off. He was sure it was about to drive away with his sister, so he started to run. The driveway was narrow and he kept to the center of it, leaving no room for a vehicle to pass. He said he was sure the car would hit him, but in the end it braked hard. Standing with his hands spread on the hood, staring his sister in the face, the engine cut off. The driver's door swept open and a man in a leather jacket climbed out, a man Eric had never seen before.

The man looked at him. After the sprint and the certainty that something was wrong, now he wasn't sure. This guy looked so...normal. Could be be one of Dad's friends or something? Eric wasn't sure what to say, and so he had defaulted to a weakly mustered "What are you doing?"

"Just going for a drive."

"Do I know you?" Eric said. "Do you know my Dad?"

"Yeah."

But he was only about five or eight years older than Eric himself. It still felt wrong. "Get out of the car, Gabby."

"Stay in the car, Gabby." The man had his arm extended in an authoritative point. Eric's eyes followed the line, and once again he realized how scared Gabby looked.

"Hey, who are you?"

"I don't think she wants to get out," he said. "I think she wants to go for a drive. Have some fun."

His face lit up in a wide smile.

"Look, I don't know you. I'm sure you think you're making a little girl's day."

"Okay, okay, I get it." He turned and walked around the trunk, hooked back to the passenger door, opened it and held it open. "Guess we can't go for a ride today."

Gabby took a tentative step out and looked up at the man, who shrugged. Seeing he wouldn't stop her, she ran around the corner of the door and right at Eric. In any other situation he might have crouched for the inevitable hug, but right now it felt too vulnerable to do anything other than stand tall. Gabby clung to his leg instead.

"I'm sorry, Eric." She started to cry. "I didn't mean to go in the car. I just wanted these. He said I could have them."

With her face still buried in the thigh of his grimy canvas work pants, she pushed her arm up at Eric, palm turned up, displaying a pair of pink plastic sunglasses. She started to shake.

"What happened?" Eric's kept his eyes on the man, who grinned and shrugged again.

"He said he was taking me on a trip," Gabby said. "He we would travel together. Forever. He said we would always be together and I would never have to come home. But I want to go home, Eric!"

Eric's face darkened. "Give me those." He took the sunglasses. "And run up to the house now. You didn't do anything wrong."

In a few moments the two of them were alone. Gabby was headed like a bullet for the house, still seemingly unable to move at anything less than a run. The man turned and shut the passenger door. Didn't say anything.

"What the fuck do you think you're doing?"

"The girl wanted to ride. Just giving her what she wants." He grinned again.

Eric took a few steps forward. "Here," he tossed the sunglasses, "take these and get off my property. Don't come back."

"Oh no, won't do that. I promise. But hey, it's a big world, right? Maybe I'll run into your sister out in it. Eric."

"If I see you anywhere near my sister, I'll—"

"You'll what?" The stranger cut him off and stepped forward. They were the same height, but Eric had never been a heavyweight.

"You'll do shit, that's what. The girl wanted to ride, Eric. She wanted it—that's what you have to get used to. They all want it. If I don't give it to them someone else will. It's not me you should be afraid of. I'm not the problem."

"You piece of shit. You come to my house—"

"She wanted it, Eric." He grinned again.

81

"—and talk to my sister—"

"She wanted to ride." He started to laugh. "They all want to ride." He threw back his head and let loose a kind of howl. "And there's nothing you can do about that."

But there was. Eric felt sure of that. Some piece inside of him sagged and gave way, soft and gentle as a sheet coming unclipped and fluttering to the ground. He hit him. Right as his laughter dimmed and his head dropped down on the level, Eric hit him right on the button, as hard as he could.

There was surprise in the man's face before he hit the ground. Eric knew the type, the kind of person who came from some bit of money, from the kind of family with time-outs instead of belts. He was the kind of guy that threatens to fight, but never does. He'd probably never been hit in his whole life.

Eric didn't come from that type of place. He hated people who did. You fire me from my job, you fuck with my sister, you come here, to my house—Eric realized he was kneeling over guy, hitting him again and again. The man was curled in fetal position. Eric kept hitting. He was crawling away towards his car. Eric grabbed an ankle and dragged him across the gravel, picked up a big rock, and stopped. Enough, he thought. Enough.

"Get the fuck out of here." Eric leaned down

and picked up the plastic sunglasses lying in the dirt and tossed them through the car window. "Don't let me see you around here again." He turned and walked toward the house. He didn't turn around.

Later, after the engine had started and the car had sped away, there was a lingering afterimage on his retina: the man on the ground, arms crossed and extended in front of him, protecting against the coming blow. There was fear on his face. But there was also something more, a hybrid of hatred and shame—shame that he was laying in the dirt taking a beating. Shame that he had been reduced in stature, and hatred for the person who had put him in his place.

The next day Eric went and tried to get his job back. The best time was between shifts. Factoring in the time it took to walk into town, he knew he wouldn't be there when Gabby got home, but he told her to go straight into the house, lock the door, and wait for him to come home. Eric wasn't rehired, and after leaving the welding shop at around three-thirty in the afternoon, he said he had taken a long walk to clear his head.

He arrived home just before six, and claimed his first sign something was wrong was discovering the bloody fillet knife on the kitchen counter. The blood was beginning to dry and to lose its vibrant red hue, so he had been unsure what it was, and picked the knife up to examine it further. Upstairs, he found the mutilated body, called 911 from the phone in the master bedroom, and tried to carry his sister downstairs to get her closer to the ambulance.

He later described the one detail that had lead him to be unable to speak when police showed up: his sister's body had been propped up in a desk chair and faced towards the door; her hair had been tied to the chair to keep her head level; on her face, covering her eyes, were a pair of pink plastic sunglasses.

Eric believed he would have reacted differently to the simple death of his sister, say in an accident, but in this case he knew that her death was his fault. It was payback, plain and simple. The display of the body, the sunglasses, were all meant as a message, a message written just for him. All the things Gabby had endured were intended as revenge, and the sunglasses were a signature.

"From him to me," Eric had said. And he had said it again and again, telling the story again and again, without ever changing a detail or getting caught in some small fabrication.

The story was compelling at trial. Eric's lawyers presented it as an alternate theory of the crime, and though the police tried and tried, there was no way to prove events didn't unfold exactly as Eric described. There were no witnesses, and the story seemed to explain all the physical evidence.

All the parts of Eric's story that could be verified were. He had been fired, he had come and tried to get his job back, but for the two hours he supposedly spent walking—the two hours during which, in the opinion of the coroner, Gabby's life had bled out of her—no witnesses or alibi could be found.

There were no witnesses to the supposed altercation the day before either. No one remembered a red Challenger driving by, or a big man in his twenties wearing a leather jacket. At trial, the prosecution emphasized that this story relied solely on the word of a suspected murderer. That was true. The defense could not produce one scrap of evidence that the man in the red car was anything other than the fabrication of a very sick mind.

The semen was typed to match Eric, but the defense was quick to point out the number of people who had the same blood type and would also be a match. In most people's opinion, not much weight was given to this evidence by the jury. The most compelling day of the trial, according to many of the journalists, was the day Eric took the stand. A murder trial is judged by the standard of reasonable doubt, and at the end of the day no one could say things hadn't happened just the way he said.

Combined with testimony that was described in more than one article as "riveting," a not guilty verdict was returned.

Some people said it was for the best, that the town needed to heal, not take revenge on a boy who'd grown up there. When the subject of justice came up, whether he'd actually done it, those same people tended to clam up. It was a sore spot that he had managed to live among them, undetected, for all those years. In their heart of hearts, most people seemed glad enough the damage had been contained in Eric's own family, and happy enough to leave it at that.

One of the more vocal locals, one who still seemed perfectly willing to lambast the Fallows clan in print months after the trial had ended, declared with some theatricality that he had "witnessed the birth of a sociopath. That boy has been nurturing a seed of something inside him for a long time, and at the end of last year, I saw it come into bloom."

At least it seemed theatrical in retrospect. Reading between the lines, one could get a sense of a town that needed to either do some serious soul-searching or forget it ever happened. Towns are like the people who live in them—most choose the latter.

ANGELA SAT BACK in her chair, unable to believe the town in the story was her town. It had been almost two years since Ted had decided he wanted to move back. She knew plenty of people who had lived their whole lives there, whose parents and grandparents had, and no one had ever breathed a word of it, as gossip or anything else. Angela supposed the story couldn't go on for ever. As far as headlines went, "Child Murderer Still On Loose" was pretty embarrassing.

But that was the gist of it: Eric Fallows was still out there. Maybe that's why no one wanted to talk about it. They were afraid to summon him, like saying Bloody Mary three times. It would be different if he was rotting in a cell; it would all be in the past. Instead the whole thing still lived and breathed in the present. Eric still lived and breathed in the present, out there in the world somewhere.

"No, not somewhere," Angela breathed. "He's here."

"He's home."

FRIDAY

OCTOBER 12TH

1990

9

ANGELA WOKE FRIDAY morning to the sound of breathing coming from behind her.

She had spent nearly three hours in the library the previous day. After driving home she had called to make sure Julie was safe, then carefully locked herself in. Special attention was paid to the new deadbolt she had installed in the door to the addition. Then she collapsed into bed.

She had nightmares, but never woke up.

When she did come around, it was to the prickle of hot breath across the back of her neck. Her stomach dropped; her eyes snapped open like over-tightened window shades. For a few seconds she couldn't move, couldn't do anything other lay on her side and stare at the wall. She was an ostrich again, head buried in the sand.

It only took a few seconds for her mind to conjure a horror tour: Eric bending over the bed, feet wrapped in garbage bags, smelling her hair; Eric wearing black leather gloves and testing the edge on a fillet knife; Eric under the covers with her—behind her—naked.

The rhythm of the breathing brought her back to reality. It was measured and slow, the breathing pattern of someone who was asleep.

Or someone who was pretending to be.

Either way, Angela realized, this was as good a chance as she was going to get. She steeled herself, then leapt up and pressed her back against the wall, twisting her head wildly from side to side, scanning the room. If someone was coming for her, at least it wouldn't be from behind. There was someone there, on the far side of the bed, rustling and...snoring. Angela picked up a small statuette with a heavy base off her bedside table, raised it over head, and—

—and realized she recognized the snoring. She reversed her weapon, used the statue side to flip back a corner of the covers.

Fucking Ted! He was here, at home, sleeping next to her. Angela remembered her certainty that Ted's return home would assuage her fears. She thought of all the nightmares she'd had, all while sleeping next to him.

"I guess it only works if I know you're there," she said out loud. And she did feel better now. The light coming through the uncovered corner of the window was bright and clear and still. Pre-hurricane weather in her experience, but even so, it was a better looking day than she had seen in a long time.

With a start, she realized it had only been three days since an almost carefree family dinner. She looked down at her husband. In some ways, she had missed him so much, needed him so much. But she had also surprised herself. She had figured out the danger to their child, figured out just how sick the man stalking their family was, and she had overcome her fear and survived. Julie was safe, the house was secure. It was only a stopgap until they could figure out what to do, but as stopgaps went she was proud of it.

She was proud of herself, and surprised at how her thoughts of Ted had diminished over the past three days. Looking down at him, she thought she would feel relief. Instead she felt...comfortable. She was comfortable now with the idea of confronting Eric Fallows alone. She would do it head-on if she had to.

Let Ted sleep. There was so much to tell him, and she doubted he would believe half of it. She also doubted her ability to unify the events of the past few days into a cohesive story, one that would make sense to him as it now made sense to her. She needed him to understand the important part: there is a monster out there, one with a penchant for young girls, and he is fixated on our daughter.

Let him sleep, and she would spend some time thinking about how to explain it all, thinking about what to do. Stepping up had given her authority, but a sense of responsibility came along with it. Ted would be thunderstruck, paralyzed. She had to be ready with their next move.

She decided to go for a hard run, across the rough terrain on the path behind her house. It was hilly, and the lull of the ups and downs, the mental energy of controlling her breathing, always freed up a part of her mind she couldn't otherwise access. Perversely, these past few days had made finding it easier. She needed that clarity now more than ever.

Ted was here, Julie was safe, and the bright still air that came only before a storm beckoned to her. There would never be a better time.

And for protection, well, nothing fazed her as long as she had Rocky.

Downstairs in the kitchen she found a note:

"Bet I'm asleep right now. Came home on the red eye hoping to beat the storm. It worked! See you soon. Love, Ted."

Angela pulled open the sliding glass door,

stepped out on the deck, whistled for Rocky, and carefully locked the door behind him. She bent over and tied the key into a shoe lace.

"Come on, boy." She started walking. Warm-ups usually lasted five minutes, but today she felt loose and ready. Today she couldn't wait. Before she hit the edge of the yard, she was running.

The trail started out flat. It was slick and colorful with the reds and oranges of damp and fallen leaves. After perhaps a quarter of a mile the hills started, small at first, bigger later. The entire area behind the house was owned by the city, but undeveloped. It extended for a few miles and then, at some invisible line, became state forest. The trees behind her house went on farther than she could ever hope to walk. She knew she should be scared to be out here, even with Rocky, but this was her territory. Besides, she had never met anyone who could keep up with her cross-country on terrain like this. Angela didn't know where it came from, but it had always been like that for her—when she wanted to, she could really fly.

Right then she kept it slow and steady, searching for that hypnotic pace. Rocky lumbered along next to her, tongue out, occasionally shooting out left or right in an attempt to corral unseen animals. At the most distant part of her usual run, the trail came around a corner and made a straight, level two-hundred-yard run just below the lip of a plateau. The path had been artificially cut level into a grade that was too steep to walk on. The result was a vertical dirt and clay wall on one side of the trail and a steep drop off into some tree tops on the other.

Coming around the corner, running along the straight-away with dry leaves curling up into the air in her wake, Angela felt better than she had in a long time. She laughed out loud. A few yards ahead of her, Rocky barked in return. Then the bark turned into that low rumble and Rocky came to sliding halt.

Angela stopped and looked down at her dog. "What is it, boy?"

She looked up at the trail again, ready to scan the area ahead, but any kind of search was a moot point.

There he was, standing in the center of the path. She hadn't so much as heard the leaves rustle. Even at fifty yards, Eric was easy to pick out. He was wearing a dark leather jacket and a pair of bright pink sunglasses.

It seemed impossible to just appear on this section of path, but Angela quickly figured he had come from above, sliding down the incline and then jumping down from the top of the vertical cut into the hill. She realized just as quickly that she couldn't escape the same way: it was effectively a wall over ten feet tall, one made of a compressed, crumbly kind of brown clay, the type that would give way at her first handhold.

But he couldn't get back out that way either. A quick glance over the steep side reinforced her first impression. As far as drops went, it was probably not survivable. This section of the path was effectively a funnel, one way in and one way out. There was only one way to go—she had to turn around, head back, run away. Her body turned halfway, and then Angela made a decision. She had been on the run from this man after their very first meeting, and ever since.

No more. Because there *was* one other direction she could go. Forward.

"Come on, Rocky." She started walking. Rocky didn't really need any encouragement. She could feel the change in his demeanor, from playful to something like human fury. She hadn't known dogs could feel that way, had certainly never seen it in Rocky, but could feel it radiating off him. Could see it, too. He was usually so clumsy for a dog, like a perpetual teenager who doesn't know how long his limbs are. In an instant he had become lithe and loose and powerful. Each footfall seemed measured, streamlined. He was, she realized, stalking.

"Good boy," she said.

Rocky didn't look up. He kept his eyes downrange, and Angela realized she should do the same. One foot fell in front of another. She started to approach. Eric's entire body was so still, it was easy to believe he had never moved at all.

That he had always been here.

Behind the pink plastic, his face was unreadable. When Angela was twenty yards out, she started talking.

"What are you doing here?" she asked, calmly as she could.

He said nothing.

"What are you doing here, Eric?"

Using his name at least got a small movement. He smiled.

"I noticed you and the dog like to come out this way for a jog," he said. "I thought it might be the perfect place for us to get together for some alone time."

Angela absorbed the crush of the emptiness around her, perceiving just how far the two of them were from anyone else. She didn't say anything.

"So, you're finally starting to put things together," Eric said.

"I know who you are. I know *what* you are."

"What am I?"

"You're a monster. Some people would say you're sick, but I have a daughter. I don't have the luxury of trying to understand you."

"That's backwards. You've got it all twisted up in your head. I'm not the dragon in this story, Angela—I'm the dragon-slayer."

"I can see why you would tell yourself that."

"I'm the one who should have recognized what needed to be done and done it," he said. "I should have done the right thing. And even though you don't deserve it, that's what I'm going to do now."

"It must make you feel better to talk like this, to rewrite everything with you as the victim, so you don't have to think about what happened to that little girl."

Eric started shaking his head. "No. You of all people don't get to talk about her."

"So you don't have to think about what you did to that little girl. To you own sister. What would Gabby—"

"DON'T YOU DARE SAY HER NAME!" It was like flipping a switch. From a default setting of cool detachment, his face morphed into a gargoyle of hatred and rage.

Angela felt herself take a step back from the sudden, near-tangible heat coming off of him. At the same time, Rocky started taking a step forward. For a second Angela thought about just letting him go, letting it happen, but instead she reached down and grabbed his collar. She could feel him surge against her, and then he was barking and snapping.

She had never seen him like this before. Rocky was a member of the family, with a seemingly human personality, but that personality had dissolved. He was all animal.

"Control your dog, Angela," Eric said.

Angela said nothing because she was putting all her energy into an act of will, forcing herself not to open her hand.

"You know, I'm glad we have this chance to talk. Just you and me. You've been reading up on me. Did you get a copy of the trial transcript too?"

"Yes," she said.

"Did you read it?"

"Yes."

"So then I don't have to tell you—you already know." The edges of Eric's eyes turned downward; a perfect mimicry of sadness. "You're not the first person to treat me like a monster. Hell, you're far from the first person to say it to my face. The funny thing is, I've never harmed another person in my whole life."

"I read your bullshit story."

"That's what it was to you? Bullshit?"

"You raped your sister and got away with it. Yes, it's bullshit." Angela half-turned, disgusted with the idea of being so close to the hands that—

"Look at me. *Look at me!*" Her eyes met his, and for second they just both just stared. "I. Never.

Touched. Her. Do you understand?" The earlier sadness returned, but this time is was mixed with his current fire. The combination distorted his features. He seemed angry and broken in a way that would be impossible to fake. Angela began to consider that he believed what he was saying and wasn't sure if that made things better or worse. A calculating sociopath was one thing, was what she had prepared herself for. An unhinged nutcase was something else entirely.

Eric perked up, smiled at her. "So now you're thinking I'm crazy."

"Either you must have done it in cold blood and planned to get away with it, or you did by accident and got lucky. And you know what? I don't care which. I really don't."

"That's good. That's progress. If you can make the leap from evil to diseased, maybe you can take a few more leaps for me."

"The police know about you. They have the locket. They found out what it is."

Eric threw back his head and laughed. "Good! I only got a glimpse of it before your loyal friend here chased me into the woods. I had a feeling that's what it was, but I didn't get a good look."

"You didn't get a good look before you buried it?"

"I've got news for you, Angela—a locket isn't

all the police are going to find."

"Yeah, they're going to find you," she said.

"Yes. Yes, they are. But not quite yet. This is the first we've had any time together, so let me tell you a little story."

"I've heard enough."

"Indulge me."

"Why should I?"

"Should I threaten you? Because I'll hurt you if you don't and blah blah blah. You could have run away the moment you saw me. Instead you're standing here. I don't need to make any threats. This moment, this is the whole reason you're still here. You want to hear what I have to say."

Angela said nothing. And inside, deep inside, she admitted that she did. So she held tight to Rocky's collar, ready to let go if the moment called for it, and started to listen.

10

WHAT DO YOU think I did after the trial ended? I tried to live, of course. Tried to re-enter my life at all the points I thought mattered, tried to forget, as though six months had just been snipped out and lost forever. I put that time into a box in my head and marked it Do Not Open. For a long time, I didn't.

My mistake was also forgetting about everyone else. I assumed they would want to forget as much as I did, that they would assist in an act of collective memory erasure by never, ever mentioning what had happened. At the time it seemed obvious. I mean, who would want to think about that if they didn't have to?

Naive, I know. Tried to get my job back, no dice. I played the pity card on that one and almost got punched in the face. To be fair, though, no one did mention what had happened. At the grocery store, on the street, it was all the same. Silence and stares. I was right about one thing—no one would mention it. But they didn't have to. I carried the whole thing around with me, throwing it on people like a bucket of cold water every time I turned a corner. I couldn't forget because they couldn't forget, and they couldn't forget because of me. It was a vicious circle.

I figure I still could have made it work. I'd lived in that town my whole life, and I don't know if even all that would have been enough for me to get the message. The message was: move on. I get it in retrospect, and I don't blame them. The truth is, they *did* want to forget. Just like me, they wanted it gone from their heads. Of course, I was the reason they couldn't make it happen, the town's dirty laundry that just wouldn't get clean. Who knows how long I would have taken it, how long I would have lived like a ghost. Probably my whole life—that wasn't the problem.

The house. The house was a problem. The second I stepped inside I could feel the slime dripping down off the walls, coming down from her room and straight through the ceiling. I spent whole days scrubbing the place at the beginning. Then I just scrubbed it once a day, then once a week. Then I gave up.

It wouldn't wash—more dirty laundry. I started sleeping in the yard, camped out in a tent next to the house, but I had to move to the barn because of the nightmares. They'd stop for a while every time I moved farther away, but as soon as I got comfortable with some new distance they'd start up again. It took a few moves for me to put that together.

When I did, I left. I'm sure people around here were plenty happy; all I cared about was putting as much distance between me and that house as possible. But there's a limit, you know. You can only go so far before you start coming back, so I had to give that up too. I still dream of the house often, but that's OK. With nightmares, I've found, the best thing to do is relax and let them happen, that way they come on slow, like good mushrooms instead of a coke-blast up the brain stem. It's like my life, you know? I live in a nightmare, every day, but you can get used to that. As long you don't fight it.

I had to give in to something else, too.

When you spend your nights dreaming of something, you spend your days thinking about it too. Given the lack of a conviction, my sister's case was still open, but I was pretty sure fuck-all was being done about it. The police knew who had done it: me. But a stupid jury had let him off, so why waste resources chasing someone who they can't touch?

If they wouldn't fix it, someone had to. I decided it would have to be me because no one else cared. So I started to read as much as I could: psychology, criminology, all of it, anything I could lay my hands on. I started investigating my own sister's murder.

But I never thought of it like that. It wasn't an investigation—it was a manhunt. I started looking for *him*.

"HE DOESN'T EXIST! Don't you get that? Even if you don't get it, I do."

Angela's voice pierced the brief pause in Eric's story. She hadn't intended to say anything at all, but the words had escaped her. It was all so…unbelievable. Rocky leaned forward, baring his teeth, chomping at the bit. Her knuckles on the hand wrapped around his collar were white.

"Oh, he exists. He is very, very real. I only said that I'm not a monster—I didn't say monsters don't exist," he said. "They do."

"I know they do."

"Really, Angela? You may think you know. You may think you understand. But you don't. You of all people, I can say with certainty, do not understand."

"Me of all people?" She was confused.

"You of all people. You, with a six year-old daughter. She's the same age as Gab— as my sister was." He looked down at his boots. "People say the world is a dangerous place, but mostly it's just filled with dangerous people. People like him."

"The man who tried to take your sister? The man with the pink sunglasses?"

"Yes."

"The ones you're wearing right now?"

"I know what it must look like to you."

Angela said nothing.

"You know, when all this started I thought you must be in on it," Eric said. "I thought no one could be stupid enough, blind enough, to be so close and yet not see."

"See what?" she asked, but he just kept talking.

"And so the sunglasses were supposed to be a message. I didn't know if they would mean anything to you, but I figured you would would pass on the message."

"What message? To who?"

"You really don't know, do you?" Eric threw back his head and laughed. His laugh was hard and deep, and somehow desperate.

"This is funny to you?" Angela asked.

"No. It's sad. It's so fucking sad, either you have to laugh or you have to cry."

"So cry."

"I haven't cried since my sister died. But I've been laughing a lot. Watching your family, hell, it's been the best time of my life in a decade."

"Why? Why us?"

"Well, not the whole family. Just one very special person."

Angela felt a cold tongue lick up her spine. Rocky must have felt it too—he lowered his center of mass and started growling again.

"If you ever look at my daughter again, I'll—I'll kill you."

Eric shook his head. "What are you doing out here? The way you kept coming when you saw me…I thought you had at least some of this figured out. You're way off. Aren't you listening? I didn't hurt anyone. I don't want anything to do with your daughter."

"Right, sure, the invisible man did it, the man no one has ever seen."

"He did do it. But he's not invisible. I found him." His eyes were glowing now, and turned upward. He looked triumphant, but also blissful, like a burden had been removed.

"After all these years," he said, "it was so easy. A simple coincidence. I don't believe in God, but sometimes little things like that make you wonder, you know?"

Rocky leaned forward.

"After all these years, I was reading the paper, an article off the wire. I think they picked it up as a human interest piece. An editor would probably call that a slow news day. For me, it was the biggest news day in a decade."

"A human interest piece?"

"About rose gardens."

"Rose gardens?"

Eric actually rubbed his hands together, jittery with an uncontainable kind of glee.

"Rose gardens, Angela. One in particular. I can pull that picture up in my head any time, it's burned in there: that face, smiling and standing next to a bunch of prickly fucking bushes. Who cares? But they printed thousands of copies, and I saw one. I recognized him right away. I can't forget that face. I see it every night when I go to sleep."

He seemed genuinely crazy now, pacing and rubbing his hands.

"And the caption! It was all so easy—revenge as color-by-number. The world doesn't work like that, Angela, it must have been the hand of something bigger than you or me. Print a picture of a murderer, then put his name right underneath it."

Rocky was getting upset, pulling at his collar, swinging left and right like a pendulum as Eric moved back and forth.

"And do you know what the caption said?" he asked.

"No."

"Guess."

"No."

"Don't worry, I know it by heart. It said: *Local gardener Ted Gray shows off his prize winning roses.*"

Angela just looked at him.

"Do you get it now? Do you understand? Your husband is a rapist and a murderer. He's a hunter, and his prey is little girls. How can you let your daughter live in the same house as him?"

Angela took a deep breath, hoping there was a way to talk him down off the mental ledge he'd worked himself onto.

"Listen, I get it. This…this thing happened, and now you're looking for someone to blame. I don't know why you picked my family, whether it's because of my daughter or something else, but you have to stop. Do you hear me? You have to stop, because we didn't do anything to you. My husband didn't do anything to you."

She summoned the courage and took a step closer to him.

"Come with me. We can go somewhere and get you some help."

"Where does he go on all those trips?" Eric asked.

"Those are for work."

"Then why can't you contact him?"

Angela wasn't sure how he knew about that. She had to stop herself from asking, prevent herself from playing into whatever fantasy he had constructed.

"That doesn't matter. He's home now, so don't try anything."

"Look at you, still protecting his every little move."

"He's my husband."

"That's the worst part. That's what makes me more sick than anything. You and the girl, you're a part of it. Without you, maybe he wouldn't be able to pull it off. Traveling the country, slicing up little girls and their families, people might get suspicious."

"Listen to yourself; he wouldn't do that."

"But no one ever does get suspicious. Why? Because when they look at him, all they see is Ted Gray, the gardener. Charming Ted, the guy down the street. Ted the husband. Ted the father."

Eric clenched his fists into two tight, white little balls.

"Don't you see? He's hiding in plain sight! And you're helping him! You're letting him do it! Without you, without Julie, he couldn't even exist!"

Tears started to roll silently down his cheeks.

"You were right—he is invisible, and you're his cover. You are. *You.*"

He was visibly shaking now, rocking back and forth, and filled with some smaller scale vibration that seemed to emanate from his core. He was a slow-motion explosion, with waves of danger rolling off him and towards Angela. Rocky felt it. His lips pulled back from his teeth and the low rumble of a growl started again, like someone had pull-started a leaf blower. But he didn't yank against his collar this time. He waited.

For a second Eric did nothing. Then he screamed, and started forward.

Angela meant for her next words to come out a yell, to be commanding. Instead, they barely escaped her lips. She rasped it, breathed it out into the world so quietly it was barely there. Just two words.

"Get him."

She let go of Rocky's collar, and he understood perfectly, launched himself across the space. She had expected that to be louder too, but the growling had stopped. Rocky wasn't wasting any time or energy on sound. He was doing only what needed to be done, no bark, all bite. It scared her, just how silent a big animal with lethal intentions could be.

And then Rocky was there there, across the space between them in a flash. At this distance his bad leg made no difference at all. Strangely, Eric was bowing, almost kneeling, coming down to meet the approaching teeth head on. At the last second, he offered his right forearm, pushing it out toward the dog's open jaws.

Rocky's teeth snapped shut on the out-stretched arm. Angela expected a kind of crunch, but instead it sounded squishy, like flopping down on an over-stuffed pillow.

She expected a scream and a yank from Eric as he tried to get away. Instead, he made no sound at all. Rocky started to pull back and forth, whipping his head from side to side, just like he would do to shake the life out of a squirrel or a rabbit. The new angles this created let Angela see the arm.

It was thicker than it should be, wrapped in some kind of protective foam. But Rocky had latched on, and didn't look like he was going to let go any time soon. It was a comforting thought: Eric might not be injured, but he was trapped.

"You know why I wanted to meet you out here?" Eric was smiling again.

"Because we're miles from anywhere?"

Eric laughed again. "Sure. That, and I knew

you'd bring Rocky here along with you. He was really giving me trouble last time I visited. People I can deal with, but dogs are tough to handle." He smiled again. "At least without a plan."

Rocky jerked back and forth and back, three times as hard as he could. It didn't seem to have any effect.

"Now, I want you to watch this," Eric said.

He turned his body and wrapped his untrapped arm tight around Rocky's midsection. It left them in a side-to-side embrace, with the other arm still firmly locked between canine incisors.

"He isn't going to let go, you know," Angela said.

"I know. In fact, that's what I'm counting on. You see, Rocky here is so very loyal to you that, no matter what, he won't let go. Without that loyalty— without that love—I could never do what I'm about to do. But his love is misplaced, just like yours. That's what makes everything else possible."

Eric started doing the one thing neither she or Rocky had suspected. Still holding firmly, he started pushing his arm instead of pulling it, forcing himself further and further into the back of the dog's mouth. He reached the back, and kept pushing.

Inch by inch, Rocky's head started to bend backwards.

"Stop it."

Another inch.

"Stop it, Eric."

Another.

"Stop it. Stop it!" Then Angela put her hands to the side of her mouth and screamed.

Rocky's ear fell flat. His eyes moved wildly. He started to whimper, but not for one second did he loosen his grip.

Angela tried to scream again, but she felt empty of breath. All that came out was dry air, a whisper, and all she could whisper was one word.

"Don't," she said.

Rocky's neck cracked like one of his soup bones.

He went limp and his eyes rolled back. Eric turned him over and stood up, brushing his hands together. Angela stood petrified, numb.

"You better run," Eric said. "There's a storm coming."

Angela looked one more time at Rocky, lying motionless, not even breathing.

Then she turned, and ran.

11

IT WAS MID-MORNING, the sun shining brightly from over-top the trees, when Angela Gray came rocketing out of the woods and across the lawn towards her house.

She was sure no one could have followed her. No one could ever keep up with her, not when she went flat out, and that was as fast as she had ever run. So she was sure there was no human being behind her, just feet away, reaching for the back of her neck. But that's how she felt, and in the madness of the moment she hadn't actually turned and looked. At the edge of her deck she stopped, took a deep breath, and snapped around.

No one.

No one behind her. She bit down the urge to laugh, to laugh in the face of her stalker. Or fate. Or God. Whoever or whatever was driving the things happening to her, Angela suddenly felt, if only for a moment, that she had the upper hand. As quickly as the moment came, it left. He could be coming around the far bend in the trail at any moment, ready to finish the job he'd started on Rocky.

Her laughter dissolved into nausea. She bent over, ready to throw up. Instead, she forced herself up the steps and over the deck, through the sliding door and into the house. The deadbolt slid shut with a satisfying thump. She turned around and pressed her face to the window. Breath came ragged and often, momentarily frosting the glass in front of her nose before letting it dissolve, rhythmically hiding then revealing the woods in the distance.

No one there.

She turned and headed up the stairs, trying desperately to organize her thoughts into something that would make sense. She should never have gone out, should never have given in to relief just because Ted was home. In the clear light of morning, everything had seemed over.

Now, it was just getting started.

Angela pushed open the door to the master bedroom, walked over to the bed, and put her hand the bulk in the center of the bed. She sank in up to the elbow. The mound was just tangled sheets and blankets. It wasn't Ted. Ted was gone.

"Ted!" She yelled in as loud as she could.

"In here, honey." The answer came from nearby. She took two steps down hall and went into Julie's room. The scene inside was a balm, soothing her with the knowledge that her family was safe and together again.

Ted was sitting on the rocking chair with Julie balanced on his knee. He looked up and smiled as Angela came into the room.

"There she is. There's Mommy," Ted said, and pointed across the room.

"Mommy!" Julie bounced down to the ground and ran over for a hug.

"She got dropped off this morning while you were out," Ted said. "I never even knew she was gone. I think I just fell into bed last night."

Angela squeezed her daughter tight and fought back tears, resisting the urge to spit everything out. No, if she had her way, Julie would never know that any of this had happened.

"What's wrong, Mommy?"

"I'm just happy to see you, baby." Angela pulled her face across her daughters jumper, wiping away the evidence of tears.

"Go play, sweetie, right here in your room. Mommy and Daddy need to talk."

They stopped right outside the room. As long as she was here, in front of the door, nothing could happen to Julie. Air poured into her lungs and she tried to find the right words. All that came out was: "He killed Rocky."

Ted's face screwed up a little bit. "What?"

"He killed Rocky. He's dead, he broke his neck." It took everything she had to control her voice, to keep it low enough that Julie couldn't hear.

"Who did? One of these assholes who race down the street? God damn it, I—"

But she cut him off as the story came pouring out, all of it, haphazard and disconnected.

"No, no, no, no, no, no, there's a man, he's been following me, following Julie, but really he's obsessed with you, he was at the supermarket and the soccer field and he was outside our house and maybe *in* our house."

"Slow down, what are you taking about?"

"And he's here—he's here, right now! He's out there in the woods, and he killed Rocky and I think he wants to kill all of us. We need to hide. We need to call the police."

"Jesus, Angela," Ted broke into a crooked smile, "is this some kind of joke?"

She took another deep breath, and for once hoped that she looked as scared as she felt. "It's no joke."

"Why would someone kill our dog? Why, for fuck's sake, why would someone be obsessed with *me*?" he said with a smile. There he was, the master of self-deprecating charm, unable to comprehend why someone would be so interested in him.

"Because he thinks, he thinks…it's a long story. But he's crazy. He's always wearing these ridiculous pink sunglasses and he said it was supposed to be some kind of message. And he was very clear on the fact that he wants to kill you."

Ted's face went pale. People use idioms like 'he went white as a sheet,' but seeing it in real life was shocking. Starting at the top of his head, all the pinks and reds of his face took an elevator trip straight down as blood drained into his neck and torso.

"Pink sunglasses?"

"Yes."

"And he's outside right now?"

"Yes!"

Ted thought for a second. "Okay, you go downstairs and call the police. I'm going to go talk to Julie and get her to hide. I'll tell her it's a game of hide-and-seek or something. Then I'm going to come down and check the doors and windows."

He took her by both shoulders. "If we're careful, no one should be able to get in, and then the police will be here. Okay?"

"Okay. It's a good plan," she said. Ted looked at her strangely for a second. Angela guessed it was because she used to just take plans like this at face value. Now she found herself unable to stop reviewing and double-checking. He disappeared into Julie's bedroom, and she could hear him starting a game of hide and seek.

It was terrifying to head back downstairs alone. If Eric was anywhere he would be down there, but Angela steeled herself for the descent. There was a plan now, a plan to save her family, and they were counting on her.

One foot fell in front of the other, silently in sneakers. She turned down the hall at the bottom of the stairs and walked into the kitchen. Through the sliding glass door she could see the woods and most of the yard.

Empty.

She kept her eyes directed out through the glass as she reached out with her arm, picked up the phone, and pressed it to her ear. A finger was already in motion heading for the nine button, when she realized there was a problem.

Nothing.

No dial tone. It wasn't a bad connection or anything like that. Instead, there was only silence. It might as well have been unplugged from the wall.

There's an energy to a piece of working technology, like it lives and breathes. Life had been extinguished here. Now all she had was a piece of heavy plastic, and the knowledge of exactly what someone means when they say their phone is dead.

"The phone isn't working!" She yelled it as loud as she could, but no one yelled back. She was about to turn and head upstairs again when something managed to catch her eye.

The light on the answering machine was blinking. She looked down the hall. Didn't see anyone. Looked over her shoulder and out through the glass door. Didn't see anyone. Hesitated, then pressed the button marked play. The tape started turning with a crackle and spit out a voice roughened and then sanded smooth by years of cigarettes.

"Hello, this is Detective Cooper. This message is for Angela Gray. Angela, please call me back as soon as you get this. I guess—" He paused. "I guess I'll go ahead and tell you on here that I got someone to take a closer look at the locket from your yard."

The tape grated and hissed.

"They compared the soil, and as far as we can tell it's the soil from the surrounding area, like from the area it was buried in. And since this case is important, we brought someone else in. Someone from the college who does digs and stuff, recovers old objects. The locket had started to oxidize, rust, and we found the by-products there in the bag with it. It was sealed, but there was probably some moisture sealed in there with it, so we're—"

A sharp hiss of static.

"—says the amount of rust is what you would expect after about ten years. And it's not just on the locket, it's in the bag too. I know this sounds crazy, but we're pretty sure that locket has been in the same place, without being moved, for the last decade. It's been in your back yard this whole time." He paused again. "He wasn't burying it, Angela. He was digging it up."

Angela watched the as the two spinning loops exchanged tape, one growing, one shrinking.

"I don't know what it means, but can you think of—"

The tape ran out, the red light turned off, the world turned sideways.

Like a jump-cut in a movie, she found herself upstairs, unsure of how she got there. She pushed open the door to Julie's room.

No one was there. She looked under the bed, in the closet, behind the drapes. She should be feeling something, she understood that much, but numbness reigned. Her heart rate didn't even feel elevated. A systematic search of the house came next. It was logical. She may not be feeling anything, but

Angela was sure she needed to find her daughter. There was no one in the master bedroom or the office, no one upstairs at all.

Down on the first floor, she already knew that the kitchen and foyer and hall were all empty. Searching the dining room and living room only took a moment, but there was no one there. Her mouth opened to call out for Ted. She stopped herself.

Could it really be that...no, she stopped that train of thought too. Whatever she felt, whatever she thought, it could all be worked out once Julie was pressed against her chest.

Only at the head of the basement steps did she hesitate. The area down there was unfinished and low, less than five feet high. It wasn't designed for people, just storage. The hesitation didn't last long; she flicked the switch and started down. At the base of the stairs, access to the rest of the space was around a ninety-degree turn. Angela put her back to the wall, took a deep breath, and peered around the edge.

A very limited number of bare bulbs cast the basement into relief, creating about equal area of light and darkness. Nothing in the light, unknowns in the shadows. She steeled herself again, then she was around the corner and out into the basement proper, lancing out in all directions, charging into corners, checking behind boxes.

There was no one there.

The cars! She sprinted up the stairs and looked out front, but all the cars were there. Now the search was taking its toll on her. She had been physically prepared to see her daughter each and every time she turned a corner. Seeing nothing each time was painful. More than that, it was confusing, because where else could they be?

And then she knew, not because it was the one place she hadn't looked, but because she could feel it in her bones. Slowly, she turned from the front window and headed down that other hallway, towards the dead end, towards the door that lead to the new addition. It should have been locked. She knew it was locked.

It wasn't. She turned the knob and stepped inside.

Hurricane Marco was getting closer, and the wind was picking up. It was whistling across the huge sheet of plastic standing in for the missing wall. The plastic was stretched taught, and under constant pressure from outside it was starting to vibrate and hum like a piano wire. There were no lights, but with a translucent wall the entire space maintained a gray and milky glow.

There was no one here either.

The door smashed shut behind her. Angela

jumped straight up and around, and there they were. Ted had his back pressed against the wall with Julie in front of him. Ted was smiling. Julie was crying, but she wasn't making a sound.

Because a hand was clamped across the lower half of her face. Even from across the room, Angela could see the fingers digging in, pushing deep into the baby fat and muscle.

"Jesus, Ted, what are you doing?"

"Gosh, I'm really sorry about this, guys. I was thinking this would never have to happen."

"You're hurting her!"

"Well, it's not like I want to, sweetheart, but sometimes we don't get what we want," Ted said.

"Just let her go, let her come over here to me, and I'm sure we can figure this out, whatever it is."

"Oh, I know we can figure it out. When life gives you lemons and all that."

She took a step forward, and Ted lifted his daughter off the ground by her head. Angela screamed.

"Let's just stop right there, okay?" he said. "I don't want us getting into the kind of scuffle forensic evidence can't explain. It's got to tell a story, you know, and a believable one. From the footprints to the blood spatter to the positioning of the bodies."

"The blood spatter—"

"Oh, fuck off, Angela. Don't pretend you don't know. If you talked to Eric about a pair of pink sunglasses then I'm sure he filled you in on the other details too. But there's no need to scare our beautiful little angel here by discussing specifics."

He reached into his outside pocket and pulled out a knife. Angela recognized it immediately. It was the fillet knife from their kitchen.

"Oh God, Ted, look, whatever happened, we can fix it. Whatever happened in the past, I don't care about it." Angela swallowed hard. "I just want my family back together."

"That's funny. You think this is a family? I guess you would. No one's beating on you, it's got to be heaven, right?"

Angela said nothing.

"That's why I picked you, you know," Ted said, "because you would be so easy to keep happy. And because I thought you would fight for—," he gestured in a vague circle at the house and at all of them with the tip of the knife, "—all this. It takes a kind of will to ignore all of the things that don't fit, all the things that don't fit into your perfect little life. Who else could I count on for something like that?"

Angela stayed rooted to the spot.

"And this little girl right here?" Ted playfully rubbed the top of Julie's head. At the same time, he pressed the point of the knife up under her jawline. "She was just a bonus."

"Why are you doing this?"

"Frankly, I never thought it would last this long. Hell, I never thought it would work this well. Ten years! The things I've accomplished—," he looked down at his daughter. "Right, no specifics. But you were both so perfect. Family man traveling on business, who would ever need to look closer?"

"What happened ten years ago?"

"Ten years ago it was my first time, and I didn't know how good it would feel. After that, I couldn't stop. Jesus," he let out a booming laugh, "I was so fucking scared afterward. I just wanted to show that little girl what was what, and then...I don't mind telling you, after I left that day, I thought I might be done."

He giggled and twisted the knife a little bit.

"I wasn't an idiot. No witnesses, no fingerprints, I was careful about that. But never— never in a million years!—did I think they would finger the brother. It couldn't have been more perfect. Honestly, I think that's what got me hooked. I've been searching for that perfect feeling ever since."

Angela felt like just lying down and going to sleep. "Ever since," she said.

"Yes, Angela, ever since. Again and again,

always trying to recreate it just so. I did learn one thing: don't shit where you eat. I got smart after that first time and never did it here again. And I went out and bought myself a nice nuclear family, just to make sure no one would ever suspect."

"And now?"

"Now, sweetheart, it's over."

"So go. Give me my daughter, and just go," she said.

"*Our* daughter, sweetie."

"Give her to me."

"Come on. You're not thinking creatively. This asshole thinks he can come back from ten years ago and fuck me? Let him try. But I'm going to flip it on him."

"You'll never be able to get away with it. The police know that little girl's locket was buried in our yard."

"So what? Crazed killer comes back to his old stomping grounds, no one knows why, but hey, he's crazy, so who can explain it? The details write themselves."

"And Julie? Me?"

"Well, it's tragic, really. On the bright side, I'm sure we'll all make the headlines. Two bodies, mother and daughter, discovered gutted. Husband's body missing, blood trail suggests he was dragged away into the woods. You don't look for someone who's already dead, especially not when there's such an obvious alternative."

"That's your plan? Rub some of your blood on the ground, everyone thinks you're dead?"

"Oh, they'll be sure, I'll make sure there's pints and pints of it, strewn all around. No one can survive blood loss beyond a certain point, so they'll be sure. It won't be mine, of course. I have a feeling," he giggled again, "that someone with my blood type will be showing up soon."

"It will never work."

"Haven't you learned anything from living with me all these years? People will explain away anything they can, any way they can. It'll work just fine. And a dead man can go anywhere and do anything, maybe even start a new family."

"A new family?" Angela felt like she was going to die just listening to him.

"Yes. A new wife. A new daughter even! I was getting tired of this one anyway." He twisted the knife again. Julie let out a muffled scream.

"Stop it! Just stop—"

"Move over towards the hole in the floor there."

"What will it take? I just want you to stop."

Ted made a ts-tsk sound with his mouth, then twisted the thin blade harder. A rivulet of blood ran down Julie's neck, and she whimpered around the edge of the hand still clamped around her mouth.

Angela started walking toward the hole cut through the wooden boards, and Ted started circling, pulling Julie along with him. He walked crab-wise, sideways, placing each foot carefully to avoid the various tools and materials strewn across the floor, always facing his wife, always keeping her daughter in full view.

Angela stopped near the edge of the hole, and Ted stopped too. His back was pressed lightly against the rippling plastic now. He took the knife away from Julie's neck and used it to point.

"I want you to get down into the—"

He was cut off by a great tearing sound punctuated by pops and pings as the clear wall ripped free of its staples. A gap appeared, and in the gap an arm. Ted's face registered only surprise as it reached down from above and latched onto the hand holding the knife. Ted sputtered, and the arm started twisting. It twisted fast and hard, and Ted dropped the knife. He let go of Julie, pushed her really, and she stumbled toward the hole.

Somehow, like she had seen Rocky do an hour ago, Angela acted on instinct and *moved*, really moved, around the gap and down onto her knees. She put out her arm, grabbed Julie, and stopped her from falling. For one beautiful second it was just the two of them, mother and daughter, looking at each other. She would have sworn Julie smiled. Then the world came roaring back up to full speed just as she had to duck.

Ted had stumbled away from the disembodied arm, and now the rest of a person had started to follow. Eric's head came through, and then his body. He forced his torso through the ever-expanding gap in the plastic wall like a baby being born. For one sweet second, Ted's face drained like a tub with the plug pulled. Then it filled with blood again, turning a red so deep it was almost purple. He grunted and started forward, only pausing to get a grip on Julie's other arm and yank her across the gap and in front of him again. This time she was between him and Eric, and Angela saw her chance. She charged, and felt a kind of elation at the release of energy it took. No more thinking, no more worrying, just forward motion, action. Ted didn't even turn to look at her.

He didn't have to, just stiff-armed her in the chest and she bounced back. Strangely, it felt like being hit with a ball of tissue paper that had been soaked in warm water. She scrabbled to unstick the wet mass from her chest, but wasn't able to. It was more rod-like than anything, and it seemed to be attached. She pulled her hand away, and it came back slick with blood.

Realization dawned slowly. There was

something sticking out of the side of her chest. An image flashed across her brain: if her torso had been a clock, a fillet knife would now be indicating approximately two-thirty. 'Morning or afternoon?' she wondered briefly, then sat down heavily on a bag of cement. She put her elbows on her knees and supported her head with her hands, which seemed to expend all her reserves. All she could do now was watch.

"Let her go." Eric's voice exploded into the confined space.

"It's nice to see you again, Eric."

"I've thought about you every day. I've thought about you more than my own sister. You're not ready for me, so just let her go."

"That's funny, I can't recall thinking of you much. So we got caught up in one little fight—I barely remember what all this fuss is about."

Eric started forward. From the small of his back Ted produced a small silver pistol.

"Turns out I did come ready after all. I want you to walk over near Angela now." The silver gun was pointed right at his chest. "You know, I wanted this to be another knife thing, because that's more your style, but it looks like you'll be changing your M.O. What the hell, it's been ten years, right? And I suppose you've really matured as a person."

Ted started circling again, closing in, forcing

him over towards the cement bags. Eric took a few steps closer, and Ted raised the gun towards him, ts-tsked again, then pressed it into Julie's temple.

"Julie, listen to me." Eric had bent down and was looking her right in the eye. "I'm going to start coming at this piece of—at your Dad, and then he's going to have to stop pointing that thing at you."

Ted's eyes narrowed. "Stop talking to her."

"He's going to have to stop pointing it at you and point it at me instead. When that happens I want you to run and hide. Do you understand? Nod if you understand."

Julie pushed against the hand and managed a small up and down.

"I call your bluff," Ted said, "you're not going anywhere."

"Ready?" Eric said, and started walking.

"Stop. Stop," Ted said. Julie tensed her body. "God damn it, stop!"

When Eric was four feet away, Ted shrugged his shoulders and raised the gun.

"Now! Run, Gabby! Run aw—"

Ted smiled, squeezed the trigger, and shot Eric in the chest. But Julie did exactly what she was told. She squirmed away, sprinted across room, and disappeared through the door into the house proper. Angela was resigned to dying, but if she had to go, she prayed this would be the last thing she would see, the last thing she would know: that her daughter had a chance again, however small.

Eric stayed standing, took one step forward, took another bullet to the chest. This one sent him slumping backwards onto the ground, until his head was propped on the cement bag next to Angela. Ted aimed carefully at his face and pulled the trigger. She wanted to close her eyes but couldn't.

The gun clicked and jammed hard with the slide back.

"Lucky for you this is a cheap piece of shit," he said. He worked the slide back and forth, muttering to himself. Eric rolled over onto his belly and started trying to pull himself up the cement bag, dragging himself over loose tools.

"You shouldn't strain yourself there, buddy. You'll just bleed out faster."

"Fuck you." Blood foamed out of Eric's mouth along with the obscenities.

"OK, I'll be back," Ted said. "Looks like this will get to be a knife thing after all. Maybe I'll run into Julie too! Don't you two go anywhere." He laughed and walked out the door.

Angela looked down at Eric. His face was down on the floor, nearly between her knees. She could only think of one thing to say.

"I'm sorry I didn't believe you."

He labored with his breath for a second, then

said: "I'm sorry I killed your dog. I just…I needed to be able to get to him."

Angela had loved that dog, shuddered, but still nodded.

"We're going to die," she said.

"Probably." Blood was frothing out of his mouth even when he wasn't talking now. "When I say so, can you flip that switch?" He used his eyes to indicate a toggle on a black box.

Angela was about to ask for what, but ended up just nodding as Ted walked back in, now holding another knife out of the kitchen block.

"So, it comes down to this," he said. "You thought you could turn your pathetic revenge fantasies into some kind of reality. And now you're—"

Eric grunted something and blood spattered across the floor.

"What was that?" Ted asked.

"I said," Eric wheezed in air before finishing his sentence, "shut up."

Ted turned red, then purple, and blew his top. "You said that to me once before, ten years ago, and I gave you what you deserved. I told you then you'd never say that to me again. Now I'm going to prove it to you."

Ted stepped over Eric's prone body. From between Ted's legs he nodded at Angela who reached out with her less-numb arm and flipped the switch. The box roared to life. From the sound of the rapid clacking she identified it as an air compressor she'd heard the contractors using.

Ted looked surprised, but put on another smile and reversed his grip on the knife so that the blade pointed down. "Whatever you're trying, it's way too late. I'm going to—"

Eric rolled off the nail gun he'd been laying on, then used the floor to lever the business end upward.

"Shut up," he said again, and pulled the trigger.

The nail shot up vertically and went through the soft underbelly of Ted's jaw and up through his mouth, neatly stapling his tongue to his brain stem. The man who had been her husband registered just a moment of confusion. Then whatever light was in his eyes went out, and he fell quietly backwards though the hole in the floor.

Angela gave some kind of mental cheer, and passed out.

12

"MOMMY, WHY DID that man call me Gabby?"

Angela was tucking her daughter into bed as the lights flickered and the wind pounded the walls outside, both heralding Hurricane Marco's imminent arrival.

The police, with Frank Cooper in the lead, had shown up about fifteen minutes after Angela gave in to unconsciousness. It turned out Julie hadn't followed instructions exactly. Instead of hiding she had run out the front door and down the street, and then another quarter-mile to the next house. The nice older lady who lived there had called the police almost immediately.

The puncture wound to Angela's torso was long but shallow. The knife had been forced in to its hilt, but the blade had ridden along the outside edge of her ribcage and stayed away from any organs or major blood vessels. After thirteen stitches—and against doctor's orders—she had checked herself out, collected her daughter, and gone home.

The new addition was sealed off by police tape, but Angela didn't want to go in anyway. She hoped the whole thing would get razed to the ground. For the time being, considering her medical condition, the police had agreed to put off the interview. She had an appointment with Frank Cooper here at the house tomorrow, and she had a lot to organize in her head, a lot to tell him.

Before leaving the hospital, she had made one visit. The room was guarded by two officers in uniform, but they knew who she was. They let her in.

Eric had been connected to a lot of tubes and monitors, but a respirator wasn't one of them. He could breath on his own, and even though they had dug one bullet out of a lung, he could talk. But Angela just looked at him.

"I don't know what to to say," was what finally came out.

"So don't say anything," he had said.

And for a long time they had sat in silence,

each thinking their own thoughts, both wondering where they might overlap.

"I think I understand everything that happened," Angela said, "but I do have one question. How did you find the locket? I mean, I know you must have dug twenty holes, but even that wouldn't be enough to find it—it was tiny."

"After I saw the article and found the house," Eric said, "I started watching. It came out earlier in the national papers. Only after they picked it up did your local paper grab it too, so I was there pretty early."

He looked off into the distance.

"And I didn't have to wait very long before I saw him bury something. You all went out somewhere that night, and I dug it up."

"The locket?"

"No. It was a bracelet, or maybe an anklet, I'm not sure. But there was a family murdered that week in San Antonio, and something similar was listed as missing."

"No, that can't be right. Look, I accept that Ted did what he did to your sister ten years ago, and he had some kind of psychotic break tonight, but in between…" Angela trailed off.

"I've been reading every paper I can for years, searching for things that smell like him. It doesn't take much effort to find one."

"How can you know?"

Eric turned and looked right at her again. "When I realized what that bracelet was, I put it back in the ground. But it gave me the idea: if he really collects mementos, and if the yard is where he keeps them, maybe my sister's missing locket would be out there too."

"And it was."

"Yes."

"But still, how did you find it?"

"When I came back the night of the last storm, I didn't only bring a shovel—I brought a metal detector too."

"Oh. But wait, it still doesn't make any sense. If you had a metal detector, then why dig twenty holes?"

"Because it kept going off, Angela. It went off again and again and again." Eric turned his head stared off into space.

"I don't believe it," she said.

"He sure did spend a lot of time out in the yard, didn't he?"

"I don't believe it."

"You don't have to. I left everything else where I found it, just kicked a little dirt on top."

ANGELA HAD LEFT then, found her daughter,

gone home and ended up here, tucking her in.

"I don't know, sweetie," she said, answering Julie's question. "He had a sister named Gabby a long time ago, and he wanted to help her. But he couldn't."

"So he helped me instead?"

"That's right, Julie. He helped you instead."

"That's good," she said, and rolled over and went to sleep.

Angela went downstairs, poured herself a drink, and stood at the glass door looking out at the yard and watching the storm. Even now, she couldn't believe it. Ted made a mistake, but it was ten years ago. He was still a human being, not some monster. She couldn't imagine leaving her daughter with a man like that, couldn't imagine *having* a daughter with a man like that. She couldn't believe it. She wouldn't.

Rain lashed hard against the glass. All over the yard, mounds of dirt were starting to dissolve. The holes were filling up with water. Something caught her eye.

Ignoring the storm, she opened the sliding door and stepped outside. Rain started coming fast down her forehead and into her eyes. Almost instantly, she had to start wiping it away. But she kept walking towards the edge of the deck, kept trying to get a better look.

There it was, right in middle of the yard. At the center of one of the holes, something was floating.

A sealed plastic bag.

She wouldn't believe it. She couldn't have been helping him all these years. A hand went to her mouth. The rain kept falling. One by one, one after another, they bobbed to the surface.

If you enjoyed Henry Carver's *Family Murders*, keep reading for an exciting preview of

DOWN TO ZERO

1

IN THE END, all they gave Laura Page was a gun and a promise.

It started at three thirty-four in the morning when the big one poked her in the side of the head. Something pinched at Laura's scalp through the covers. She tried to shake it off but it wouldn't let go. It felt like her hair was caught in the baseball cap she liked to wear out in the park or to the beach. Pulling it off, the cheap plastic strap would inevitably take a few long, blond hairs along with it. She'd give a little yelp and Ben, her son, would giggle. Mark would kiss her and ask her if she'd ever learn her lesson.

Still four out of five parts asleep, Laura reached

up to disentangle herself from whatever had hooked her hair. Her fingers drifted sleepily up the sheet, across the pillow, and touched something warm and soft and solid. Her hand snapped back and she froze, still buried under the blanket.

She blinked in the darkness. Whatever it was, it had felt like flesh. Like an arm.

Ben, playing a joke on her? Probably Mark, trying to get her attention. But both of them were gone. The house was empty. She gave a quick shake of her head and felt the sharp pinch spread across her scalp.

Her hair was definitely caught in something. It made no sense. She reached out again, slowly, sure there must be some mistake.

A man's thick, calloused hand locked around her wrist just as the light clicked on.

Laura's heart exploded into a flutter in her chest and she screamed. Her mind, racing, could only take in the barest impressions of the man in front of her.

Big. That was the first word to spring into her mind.

Then: *ugly.*

He had a nose the size of a golf ball, pock-marked like craters on the surface of the moon. Eyes that seemed small and beady in comparison. He grinned a mouthful of yellow teeth at her. Laura screamed again, and he jumped on top of her.

The impact of his body drove all the air out of her lungs in a great whoosh, compressing her torso until every bit of it had left her body. Still the man pressed down on her, relentless. Her mouth made sucking noises. Blood began to throb in her temples.

Air. She needed air.

So close to all that oxygen filling the room, Laura felt she could taste it. But hard has she tried, her lungs could not expand. As her legs kicked and jerked under the covers, an exquisite awareness descended on her. She tuned in to breeze slid wastefully up and down her shins, making her flesh prickle. All that air and she couldn't get a bit of it.

A creeping stain of blackness bled into the edge of her vision.

"Enough," an accented voice said.

The big man spent another few seconds with his face buried in her hair, then climbed up off of her. His hands ran down her body in the process, lingering between her legs a moment longer than they had to.

Laura's lungs expanded and she drank the air in great desperate gulps, sounding for all the world like an asthmatic recovering from an attack. The smell of the ugly man hit her like a blow—body odor mixed with cheap, alcoholic aftershave—and as her breath calmed down, her mind began to race again. All the questions, forgotten during her desperate need for air, flooded back in.

Who were they? How did they get in the house? What did they want? Mostly, she thought of Ben.

"Unpleasant, no?"

Laura took one more deep breath and looked. In the corner, her wing-back reading chair held a smaller man with one leg hooked over the other, his fingers folded over his knee. His frame was narrower than the ugly man, just as tall but with a thin, whippy build. He had a thin mustache and deep tan color to his skin that made him seem Spanish or perhaps South American. When he spoke his English had a slight accent, and even bathed in a dim forty watts from her shaded reading lamp, Laura could tell he was very good looking.

He stayed silent for a beat, lips pursed, before beginning to speak.

"I am Talal. This charming gentleman is Witz. Scream again and Witz will sit on you again. That is not my wish, but a necessity if you cannot control yourself."

"My husband will be back any second," Laura said.

Talal smoothed his silk tie and shook his head. "I think not, Mrs. Page. Mark is out of town. Why do you think we picked tonight to visit you?"

Laura's next threat, already barreling up out of

her, caught in her throat. Her mouth hung open.

"And don't worry about Ben," Talal said.

Ben. Ben. Ben Ben Ben. Her son's name bounced around inside her head like a pinball. It had all happened so fast—where was he? Did they have him?

"Ben is safe, Laura. May I call you Laura? He is at a sleepover tonight, remember?"

Relief sagged her body for a moment, then dread propped it up again. "How do you know where my son is?"

"Because we have been watching him, Laura, just as we have been watching you. We watched you drop off Mark at the airport. We watched you drop off Ben at his sleepover. We watched you come back here all alone to a half bottle of wine and cheap television in your very thick-walled house. They used to build houses to last, Laura. How old is this one? A hundred years?"

Laura said nothing, just pulled the sheet up to cover her body. Witz frowned an ugly frown at her. He looked disappointed.

Talal leaned toward her. "No one heard you scream, Laura. No one is coming. Do as we say and everything will work out, okay?"

The blood still rushed in her ears. She looked from Talal to Witz and back again. What else could she do?

She nodded.

"Here," he stood from the chair, buttoned the top button of his suit jacket, and extended his hand, "shake on it."

Laura waited for him to come over but he made no move. She got up, clutching the sheet around her. Witz's eyes—she could feel them all over her. Talal, though, looked right into her eyes, never letting his eyes wander down across her body. She took his hand. It felt soft. Not too dry, not to moist. Perfectly manicured.

He squeezed her hand and moved the whole assembly up and down for the both of them. "I have your word, then?"

Could she still be dreaming? It seemed like a dream.

He released his grip, dropped his hand, and twisted his hips. Then he twisted them back again, bringing his hand across at the end of his arm like a weight on the end of a chain. The back of his hand connected full-force across her cheek.

She fell to one knee. The side of her head felt like it had cracked. Her vision went white for a second, then came back blurred.

Talal grabbed her around the throat, pulled her to her feet. "Your word, Laura. Your promise. Do I have it?"

The tears started then, some invisible dam

shattered by the blow. They ran hot and silent down Laura's face as she choked.

They made her dress in their presence, made her walk down the stairs in front of them and then lead them into the garage. First Witz got into the back of her BMW, right behind the driver's seat. Then she climbed behind the wheel. Talal gave a small bow and shut the door for her, an act of perfect chivalry.

A greasy set of fingers reached around the headrest and started twisting some of her hair. Witz inhaled audibly through his great big nostrils. "God, that smell. You have the most beautiful hair. Nothing like beautiful hair on a beautiful woman."

His breath stunk like garlic and coffee. The other rear door opened and Talal scooted across the leather and tapped her on the shoulder.

"Oh driver."

She turned and looked at him, eyebrows furrowed, trying not to panic.

"Take us away," he said.

The key turned and the engine sprang to life. Witz's fingers touched her just below the collar bone.

She gritted her teeth. "Where am I going?"

"To work, Laura," Talal purred. "You're going to work."

Ryan Macklin has a problem: he's an addict. A tour in Afghanistan claimed his leg and left him hobbled in more ways than one. Now clean for more than a year, Mack wants nothing more than the quiet life. He works at the Manhattan VA, cares for his paraplegic sister, and most of all wishes he could silence his demons.

Across the city, a handsome foreigner cuts a bloody path through midtown Manhattan, employing a mix of precision and extreme brutality in pursuit of a mysterious briefcase. More death is in the cards as long as he can keep to a very strict schedule.

Only Mack is on a collision course. Now he must fight to stop a mad man, to uncover a sickening secret, and to grab hold of one last chance at redemption.

Down to Zero: A Thriller,
available now.

5235407R00090

Printed in Great Britain
by Amazon.co.uk, Ltd.,
Marston Gate.